JUSTICE

FINDS HER WAY HOME

THE ULTIMATE CHALLENGE COMES FULL CIRCLE

TINA TENNYSON

Inspired Forever Book Publishing
Dallas, Texas

Inspired Forever Book Publishing™
"We Bring Inspiration to Life"
Dallas, Texas
(888) 403-2727

Printed in the United States of America

Library of Congress Control Number: 2018933146

Softcover ISBN-13: 978-0-9996258-2-8

DEDICATION

This is dedicated to all of the women that have been missing, murdered, or unclaimed. Though there are so many things that have attempted to restrict women of color, we rise with impeccable grace.

ACKNOWLEDGEMENTS

I would like to thank my loving family and husband for their support. This would not have been possible without your encouragement. I also want to thank my publisher and editor for dealing with my highs and lows on this project. And lastly, I want to thank all of the assorted people who have come in and out of my life over the years. I am a better person because of my experiences with you all.

TABLE OF CONTENTS

PROLOGUE

Walking through the parking lot, Manolo Blahnik suede pumps clicking against the asphalt, Naomi Tanner whistles an earworm she hasn't been able to shake for several hours. Her mind is on the surprise dinner plans her husband told her he'd made for the two of them.

I wonder what he has up his sleeve, she thinks.

Arriving at her car, a midnight blue BMW, she's reminded of the perks that go along with being married to a professional football player. Her reflection in the window catches her eye. Business casual slacks, a black silk Stella McCartney top, and a purple blazer. Hmm . . . this outfit will never do for a romantic dinner. And something's missing. Her lunch case.

"Damn it," she mutters under her breath. She turns on her heels and heads back through the parking lot. The early evening sun is warm, and she can feel the first beads of perspiration on her brown skin. She notes that only five or six cars remain.

He might be aggravated that I'm late, but I'm sure I can figure out *something* to make him not be so angry with me, she tells herself, adding a provocative wiggle to her walk at the thought of her evening ahead.

On the inside of the six-story building, she gives a brief wave to the security guards, mouthing the words, "I left something in my office." The two guards briefly acknowledge her, too deep in their own conversation to care.

The elevator is a vacuum of body odors and perfumes, and she is thankful the ride is a short one. Still whistling, she checks herself in the gold-rimmed mirror mounted inside the elevator. As the doors part and she turns left toward her office, she remembers seeing Michelle Greeley's car in the parking lot. Wondering what her best friend is working on this late, Naomi decides to stop by Michelle's office to gloat about her date night with James.

Three doors down from Michelle's office, Naomi takes off her heels so that she can sneak unnoticed toward her friend. Michelle is one of the operations supervisors for the company and is pretty damn good at her job. With so few black faces among the management at this company, the two women gravitated toward each other. Rather than chew each other's heads off fighting for the most power, the women chose to help each other get to the top, and it was this shared strategy that solidified their friendship almost from the get-go.

Naomi hears noises as she leans against the wall to take off her other shoe. Is she really hearing this? Panting and whispers are coming from Michelle's office. Barely realizing both shoes are off her feet and in her hands, Naomi inches down the hall toward her friend's office, attempting to be as quiet as a mouse. One door. Two doors. The third door is Michelle's and it's partly cracked. Not enough for Naomi to be seen but enough for her to see inside. Approaching the opening in the door, Naomi peers inside to see her friend of five years bent forward over her desk, dress up. A man is standing behind her, slacks around his ankles, thrusting hard.

"Tell me you love me." The male voice sounds hoarse and breathless.

"I love you," Michelle responds, in a barely audible whisper.

He's stroking her harder now, and Naomi hears her friend whimper softly. Suddenly, the man, whose face Naomi can't see, begins choking her friend. Naomi's heart rate quickens. She's compelled to intervene until she realizes her friend isn't struggling. Quite the contrary. The chokehold is just enough to bring a rise in Michelle's climax. Naomi stands in the doorway, both shocked and turned on by what she sees. She can't bring herself to walk away from the doorway. She wants to know who the mystery lover is.

His thrusting quickens, and Michelle, clearly at wit's end with pleasure, can stifle her screams no more. In the heat of passion, she becomes more vocal, screaming out, "Jason!"

Naomi's eyes widen. Jason Smith is one of the people who reports to Michelle on her team. A smile curls on Naomi's lips. So this is why Michelle has been canceling drink nights after work! It has nothing to do with keeping up with deadlines! Well, I'll leave them to clean up, Naomi thinks, tiptoeing back to her office.

Reaching her office, shoes still in her hand, Naomi grabs her lunch case and heads back out the door, which is only four doors down from Michelle's. She closes the door quietly behind her, locking it with a key. She hears the sound of glass breaking from Michelle's office. Not sure what to expect, she heads back down the hallway. Michelle's door is closed tightly. They couldn't have made it to the elevator that fast without being seen. Naomi knocks. No response.

"Michelle, are you in there? It's Naomi." Still, no response.

Naomi knocks once more and listens closely for any sound in Michelle's office. Hearing nothing, she heads for the elevator. "Guess I somehow missed them," she says to the empty hallway.

It's no wonder to Naomi why her friend would take a lover. Michelle's husband is the vice president of the company and a pompous asshole. Norman Greeley is not only cruel to his wife; he also has a flock of women he attends to whenever his mood suits it. At forty-eight, Norman still has the looks and the income to attract both younger women and his contemporaries. Good for her, Naomi thinks on the elevator ride back down to the lobby. Passing by the security guards, who are still deep in conversation, she bids them a final farewell with a knowing nod. Based upon the events she'd just seen, she can only imagine what has them so deeply enthralled in conversation.

Walking to her car, shoes still in hand, she begins to whistle again. Throwing her lunch case, shoes, and purse onto the passenger seat, she drives home with thoughts of her own sexual adventure on her mind.

With memories of a wonderfully romantic evening with her husband still playing on an endless loop in her brain, Naomi is in a wonderland of daydreams the next morning at work and doesn't notice Michelle entering her office until she is sitting directly across the desk from her.

Naomi's smile quickly fades into a look of complete shock when her eyes meet Michelle's. Michelle is wearing way too much makeup. And it's doing nothing to mask the bruise under her left eye. Naomi's thoughts return to the sound of glass breaking the night before.

At Naomi's astonishment, Michelle launches into ordinary work chatter. Who's sleeping with whom; who got caught stealing office supplies. But Naomi can't hear her this morning. She can see Michelle's mouth moving but is completely deaf to the sound.

"What happened to your eye?" Naomi asks, attempting to sound matter-of-fact.

Michelle stops talking immediately and sits back in her chair, appearing to carefully weigh her words.

"Oh nothing, girl. You know how Norman can be sometimes." Then she moves back to the conversation she started without any hesitation.

All Naomi can think about is the broken glass from the previous night. She can only shake her head and nod at the stories coming from Michelle's mouth. What happened in that office last night? Did Michelle and Jason fight? Did hot sex turn into a heated argument? Did Norman catch them? So many questions run through Naomi's mind. But she says nothing and Michelle doesn't acknowledge her quietness. Once she finishes whatever juicy gossip she has to say, Michelle gets up and walks out of Naomi's office without another word. As if nothing has happened at all.

Naomi sits at her desk in a haze, wondering if she should have said anything about Jason.

CHAPTER 1

The summer sun pours into their bedroom window and ignites the gold duvet covering their king-sized bed. It's Saturday morning, and Naomi peers out from under the covers. Her husband's side of the bed is empty. He always was an earlier riser. Wearing one of James' old college t-shirts, Naomi flips the covers back. Before she can get one foot on the floor, she hears the shower water running and a knowing smile spreads across her face. But there isn't time. She can hear two tiny humans running down the hallway making their way toward her bedroom. Three-year-old Daniel and two-year-old Serena burst through the doorway.

"Good morning, Mommy!" they greet her in unison.

"Good morning, babies! What do we want for breakfast this morning?" Naomi hears the shower in their master bathroom turn off, and before she can get out of bed, both children climb up on each side of her.

"We want Cheerios for breakfast!" they exclaim once again in unison.

"Sounds like a great breakfast to Mommy! Go downstairs and sit at the table and Mommy will come make cereal." She

7

can't help but smile. At twenty-nine years old, she already feels like she has it all.

"OK, Mommy!" Daniel says, jumping down off the bed. "Race you downstairs, Serena!"

Daniel is already running down the hallway of their two-story Colonial-style home, and Serena's little legs do all they can to catch him as he navigates the stairs and races past the living room.

"Be careful you two! I don't want either of you hurt!"

A unison "yes ma'am" echoes through the stairwell.

In that moment, the master bathroom door opens, revealing James Tanner's muscular, towel-wrapped body. Naomi surveys his entire physique seductively. Damn. The gym has definitely been good to him. They met in college when James was finishing up his senior year and Naomi was a sophomore. From the moment she first met him, Naomi couldn't take her eyes off of him. Now a linebacker for the Detroit Lions, James, at six-foot-five, is one stocky hunk of delicious man. His brown skin glistens with water droplets. His hazel eyes lock with hers. James walks toward their bed, leans down, and places the lightest kiss on Naomi's lips before whispering into her ear.

"Five-minute quickie before you make cereal for the kids."

Naomi can faintly hear the kids playing downstairs. Plenty of time for a quickie. With a spark in her deep brown eyes, Naomi leans back on the bed. Before "yes" can escape her lips, James leans in, unwraps the towel, and lifts up the college t-shirt—one of his favorites—covering his wife. Almost instantly, he's inside her. Naomi exhales, reminding herself that the kids are downstairs and any amount of noise will send them running up the stairs to investigate. Looking deep into her eyes, James creates their rhythm. Running his fingers through her curly brown hair, he speeds up the pace, gripping handfuls of her locks as he stifles his own groans. Panting and moaning as lightly as possible, they climax together.

"Looks like you need another shower, Mr. Tanner."

"Mommy, what's taking you so long?" It's Daniel's eager voice from the bottom of the stairs.

Naomi jumps up from the bed and runs into the bathroom to wash up and slip into some shorts. When she comes out of the bathroom, James is still lying across the bed.

"Duty calls, my love." She leans in and kisses him before heading downstairs.

Rounding the corner into their upscale kitchen, she smiles warmly at the sight of her two kids seated like angels at the marble-topped island.

"All right, you two, it's time for Cheerios." Naomi beams at a minutes-ago memory while she grabs two bowls and the box of cereal from the cabinets. She doesn't notice James' cell phone at the end of the island until it begins flashing. Daniel and Serena are still completely distracted, playing innocently with two action figures that have seen better days.

Flashing on her husband's screen are these words followed by a wink emoji: *Dominique: I had a great time with you last weekend. You should really keep in touch!*

Total and complete shock washes over Naomi. Her legs feel numb. Daniel's voice interrupts the onslaught of questions racing through her head.

"Don't forget to put extra milk in my cereal, Mommy, so I can grow up big and strong!" Daniel makes the muscle arms he has practiced a thousand times with James.

She is forced to collect her thoughts and shove them into the darkest regions of her mind. Putting on her best smile, she shifts her attention back to her kids.

"Mommy won't forget the extra milk in your cereal, Daniel."

"Me too! Me too!" sings Serena.

"You too, Serena." Naomi only pretends to pour extra milk in Serena's cereal. At two years old, Serena's lucky if half the milk makes it from spoon to mouth. Turning her back toward the kids to put the milk away, Naomi closes her eyes and holds her breath for ten seconds. When she turns back around, she sees two tiny people stuffing Cheerios into their mouths, and all is right in the world again. At least for breakfast.

CHAPTER 2

Sitting at her desk, staring off into space, Naomi contemplates all of the events that have taken place in the last couple of weeks. Not just with herself; she is worried about Michelle as well.

She hasn't confronted James about the text message from "Dominique" she saw on his phone a couple of Saturdays ago. And she hasn't mentioned it to Michelle. Instead, Naomi has turned her full attention to work and their children. She isn't sure how she wants to handle her situation with James yet. Still deeply hurt, she has the needs of her children to consider.

The bruising around Michelle's eye has gradually improved, and only a faint discoloration remains around her bottom lid. Naomi never did get the details on what really happened to Michelle that night. But it wasn't for lack of trying. Michelle was just better at evading questions than Naomi was at asking.

This morning was identical to most of their mornings together. Still staring at her computer screen, Naomi doesn't look up when Michelle opens her door and invites herself to sit in her usual chair, across from Naomi's desk.

"Well good morning, sunshine! You look deep in thought today!"

"Yeah, a lot going on as usual. Fill me in on the gossip so I can be distracted by other people's bullshit."

Michelle laughs and starts rambling about office drama involving everyone but herself. It's a tactic, Naomi decides, to keep the spotlight off of Michelle's personal life. Though Naomi isn't listening, she is grateful to her friend for the meaningless distraction. The sound of Michelle's voice and the normalcy of their morning routine are both comforting. After her usual ten to fifteen minutes of idle chatter, Michelle gets up from the chair.

"All right, girl. These reports aren't going to write themselves. And before you ask, no drinks tonight! I have been completely swamped with work lately."

Naomi pouts playfully.

"Don't give me that face! Drinks are coming soon. I have so much to tell you, and I'd rather do it at a bar," Michelle winks as she closes the office door behind her.

Naomi's curiosity is peaked. She'd better be telling me about her new love affair with Jason! Shaking the thoughts from her head, Naomi dives back into her work.

Another long workday is coming to an end for Naomi, and she calls the daycare center to make sure that Imani—a local college student who helps Naomi with the kids—has picked up the children so she doesn't have to. A hectic pre-season training schedule keeps James far too busy most days to help out. Confirming that her babies have been safely picked up and are on their way home, Naomi decides to check in on Michelle to see if she is actually doing work this time around.

Naomi knows the answer before she even reaches her friend's office. The sounds of lovemaking and desktop items being displaced can be heard through Michelle's door, which is tightly closed this time.

It's six thirty when Naomi reaches the parking lot. So few cars remain that it's painfully obvious who is still inside the building. Michelle really needs to be more discreet. Jumping into her car, Naomi heads home to prepare her family for another day.

"Count On Me" by Bruno Mars plays over and over again, vibrating the nightstand by the bed. Naomi stirs slightly.

"If you ever find yourself stuck in the middle of the sea, I'll sail the world to find you. If you ever find yourself lost in the dark and you can't see, I'll be the light to guide you."

Naomi jolts upright, suddenly realizing it's the ringtone she assigned to Michelle's number. Completely disoriented, she fumbles for her phone in the darkness. James stirs but only to get more comfortable in the bed.

Finding her phone, Naomi presses the home key. The time reads 2:30 a.m., and she has ten missed calls from Michelle in the last thirty minutes. Calling her back, Naomi receives no answer. Whatever she has to tell me can wait 'til work tomorrow, she thinks groggily. Plopping her phone back on the nightstand, Naomi snuggles up against James and drifts off to sleep.

Sitting at her desk, staring at her computer like every morning, Naomi waits for Michelle to walk into her office. But Michelle is late. Thirty minutes beyond her usual arrival time pass, then forty-five. An hour and a half into their workday there is still no sign of Michelle. Damn it, Michelle; today is not the day to play hooky and not tell me about it.

Naomi pulls out her cellphone and presses Michelle's name to call her. It goes straight to voicemail. Now completely puzzled, Naomi gets up from her desk and steps out into the hallway on a mission to find answers. She sticks her head into the office next to her.

"Amanda, have you seen or heard anything from Michelle this morning?"

"No, sweetheart, I haven't. I was just about to come into your office and ask you the same thing. She was finishing up a report last night, and I need it for a meeting this morning. She didn't email it last night."

"Well, let's get security to let us into her office so you can get what you need. And just maybe there will be something on her calendar saying where she is today. Her cell is going straight to voicemail."

Taking the elevator to the first floor, Amanda and Naomi walk up to the security desk. Andre is on duty.

"Well good morning, sir. Can you do us a favor and let us into Michelle's office? Amanda needs some work off her desk and so do I. Pretty please?" Naomi bats her eyes.

"Anything for you, Naomi," Andre smiles, his baby face punctuated by the cutest dimple in his right cheek that belies his late-twenties age. At about five-nine, Andre looks like he hits the gym several times a week. I'm married, not blind, Naomi thinks. And besides, a little eye candy can help a girl through a long day at work. Naomi often sensed that Andre had a little crush on her, and needing access to Michelle's office, Naomi is more than willing to exploit those feelings now.

"Thank you! We appreciate you!" Naomi flashes her smile.

Amanda rolls her eyes at their playful flirting.

With a set of keys in his hand, Andre leads the way back up to Michelle's office. Naomi is suddenly aware of how anxious she is to see what's inside. The sounds of lovemaking she heard the evening before echo in her mind. She's overcome with guilt, as if they're entering someone's bedroom without permission.

As soon as the door opens, it just doesn't feel right. The blinds are drawn so there isn't much light in the room. Andre flips on the light switch and all of their jaws drop to the floor. It looks like a tornado has hit Michelle's office. Papers are everywhere. Furniture is turned over. The three exchange looks. Without thinking, Naomi approaches her friend's desk, looking for anything that might help make sense of the mess. The papers littering the top of her cherry desk and her leather office chair are peppered with dark drops of blood. Amanda and Andre are frozen in the doorway.

"Ladies, touch nothing! We need to leave this office right now. I have to report this and, Naomi, you never entered this office. Are we clear?"

Andre's tone sends a chill down Naomi's spine, as she turns on her heels quickly to face them. "I was never in here."

CHAPTER 3

Naomi watches from her office window as four squad cars containing members of Detroit's finest police taskforce file into the parking lot. Her heart begins to race as the truth starts setting in. Michelle is dead or very badly injured. But where is she? Her mind is so clouded by questions and fear that Naomi—now sitting at her desk—doesn't even remember stepping away from the window. She isn't surprised when there's a knock at her door twenty minutes later.

She shouts, "Come in," as she turns toward her door. It's Andre. And he has a very serious look on his face. Naomi braces herself.

"The police are asking to interview everyone in the office, whether you have a working relationship with Michelle or not. They will start to question the security staff first and then work their way up. Just wanted you to be prepared for questioning."

"Thanks for the heads up, Andre. You're sweet." Trying hard to look busy, Naomi ruffles some papers on her desk, giving Andre his queue to exit.

"I will leave you to your work then," he says, taking the hint.

The investigation has clearly stirred excitement and speculation, as office doors that are normally closed are now open, and hushed conversations can be heard emanating from groups of curious employees. Crime scene analysts are in Michelle's office searching for clues, and at the end of the hall in a conference room, interviews are taking place.

The pit of Naomi's stomach feels sour. Eavesdropping on Michelle's lovemaking is not something she wants to admit to a team of investigators. Naomi reluctantly opens her office door as well—a subtle message to everyone in the hallway that the investigators will have her full cooperation. It's stuffy in here anyway, she tells herself.

Everyone in the office knows that Naomi and Michelle are thick as thieves, and as soon as Naomi opens her door, all eyes turn in her direction. Ignoring the stares, Naomi quietly leaves her office and heads for the ladies' room. She can hear the chatter resume once the door closes behind her.

Staring in the mirror, Naomi flashes back to a time of innocence, when her most difficult choice was whether to wear white or pink bobby socks with her black patent leather shoes. There is one day in particular that Naomi will never forget as long as she lives—one profoundly tragic day when innocence left.

She was sitting in Mrs. Peterson's third-grade class in her white uniform shirt and navy blue pleated skirt. It was "silent reading time," just like they had every day for half an hour. The familiar tap on her shoulder signaled her that Briana, her best friend since kindergarten, was passing her a note and attempting to go unnoticed by Mrs. Peterson's watchful eyes. Naomi pretended to accidentally drop her pencil on the floor as she collected the note, lying a few inches to the right of her backpack. Noticing the disruption, Mrs. Peterson's eyes questioned Naomi's movement.

I dropped my pencil, Naomi mouthed.

Nodding her head, Mrs. Peterson put her nose back in her own book—probably some disgusting romance novel, Naomi thought.

Naomi unfolded the note as slowly and as silently as possible.

Meet me at our favorite tree.

A smile appeared on Naomi's face as she envisioned their favorite tree where she and Briana had carved their initials with their school scissors one afternoon on their walk home. It was Briana's idea. She said that carving their initials meant that they were best friends forever. The tree was only a block away from the school; they had to pass it every day on their way home. Most days, they stopped at the tree to rub their fingers across their initials, giggling and playing around the tree for only a few minutes. Sometimes, they even shared a secret or two, maybe about a sibling getting on their nerves or someone at school they had a crush on.

When school finally ended that day, Naomi picked her way through the crowd of students, all suddenly energized by the final bell. She stuffed her school supplies in her locker and grabbed the jacket her mother had insisted she bring that day, even though the weather was warm. She slid her arms inside the jacket and then had the urge to use the restroom before meeting Briana. Naomi took her time, knowing that Briana would wait patiently for her at the tree. Neither of them was allowed to walk home alone.

Leaving the restroom, Naomi walked down the hall and stepped out of the building and into the sunlight of the day. She definitely didn't need her jacket. Naomi stopped and took off her backpack and stuffed the jacket inside, then resumed her walk toward their special tree. Oddly, Naomi could see from a distance that Briana wasn't there. Once she reached the tree, Naomi rubbed her fingers across her initials like she always did, then over Briana's as well. She stood there and waited anxiously, looking at every group of kids that passed by in hopes of spotting her friend. After what felt like forever but in reality was twenty minutes, Naomi started to walk home. She knew her mother watched the clock closely and would be worried if she were more than a few minutes off schedule. Naomi walked as quickly as her third-grade legs would take her. She reached her front door slightly out of breath. Her mother opened the door before Naomi could even grab the knob.

"Just where have you been, young lady? You should have been here ten minutes ago."

Still panting slightly, Naomi spoke. "Waiting for Briana at our tree, Mommy. But she wasn't there."

Her mother, Cynthia, stepped away from the doorway to give Naomi room.

"What do you mean?"

"I waited for her by our favorite tree and she never came."

With a concerned look on her face, Cynthia went to the phone on her kitchen wall and dialed a number.

"Hey, Robynne, I know you're just getting home but has Briana made it home yet?"

Hanging up the phone, Cynthia's eyes looked bewildered. She grabbed Naomi's hand and guided her through the front door and to the car that was parked on the side of the house. They drove two cross streets away from their home before Cynthia finally spoke again.

"Did you see Briana at all after school today?"

"No, Mommy. I had to pee after school so we didn't walk out together. But she told me in class to meet her at the tree."

Stopping in front of the Anderson's house, Cynthia gripped the steering wheel tightly. Moments later, Robynne Anderson emerged from her house, rushing down the few stairs that led from her front door and hopped into the car on the passenger's side.

Her voice was high-pitched and frantic. "Are you sure you didn't see Briana after school?" She turned and looked at Naomi sitting in the backseat.

"No, ma'am." Naomi lifted herself from the back seat and handed Robynne the folded note Briana gave her earlier in the day.

Gripping the note, Robynne opened it. Cynthia began to drive again. After thirty minutes, the car stopped and they got out. Cynthia held Naomi's hand tightly as they proceeded down the sidewalk to a building that had a sign in front that read, Detroit Police Department. The three of them rushed inside the building to a small, chaotic waiting area. Naomi could hear phones ringing amid the mindless chatter going on around her. She stepped aside as a police officer hurried by.

Robynne approached the main counter with Cynthia close by her side. Naomi was too small to see over the counter, but if she stood on her tiptoes she could see the top half of a white man's face.

Robynne's voice was frantic. "My daughter didn't come home from school today!"

Never looking up, the officer spoke. "Has the disappearance been twenty-four hours or longer?" He seemed annoyed at their interruption.

"No, but," Robynne started.

"There is nothing we can do until twenty-four hours have gone by. I'm sure your daughter will turn up. Come back tomorrow if she still hasn't shown up."

Naomi watched the officer's eyes. He continued looking down.

"In twenty-four hours she could be dead!" Robynne screamed.

"I said, come back tomorrow." The man's voice was more commanding than empathetic.

Robynne slammed her hands on the desk. "Tomorrow will be too fucking late!"

The officer started to rise, and Cynthia grabbed Robynne's arm.

"Let's go," Cynthia nudged gently. "Maybe she's already home."

Naomi never forgot that car ride home and the silence that hung heavy and stagnant.

In the coming days, Naomi helped her mom and Robynne hang posters with Briana's picture. The police it seemed, without any witnesses or leads, had no trail to follow. And from what Naomi overheard her mother saying to other mothers, the police didn't seem to be looking that hard, either.

Two weeks after her disappearance from the school grounds, Briana's body was found in an abandoned building.

The police didn't help then, so why should I rely on them now? Naomi asks her reflection, coming back to the present day. In that moment, she decides it's up to her to bring Michelle's attacker to justice. She had been too young to help Briana, but now, she's not going to let anything stand in her way of helping Michelle.

Composing herself, Naomi does her best to appear OK, even though she is far from it, and bravely exits her temporary solitude.

Feeling an overwhelming urge to be near Michelle's office, Naomi walks toward her friend's open office door. One investigator is taking photos while another is putting what must be some sort of evidence into a clear plastic bag. She heads back to her own office with all of her coworkers watching her every move. She sits behind her desk, door still wide open, not inviting anyone but not rejecting anyone's company either.

As the workday comes to an end, most of the office doors are now closed and just about everyone is gone for the day.

Naomi feels a sense of relief. The police didn't get around to interviewing her yet, and they've packed up most of their things from Michelle's office. Somehow, none of this seems quite real to Naomi. She realizes that on some level she'd been holding out hope all day that Michelle would waltz into her office and say the whole thing was a big misunderstanding. Gathering her emotions, she makes a phone call.

"Hey Imani, can you grab the kids from daycare for me? I'm running late again tonight. Thank you so much sweetie! There is meatloaf in the fridge you can heat up for dinner. And can you do me a huge favor and make sure they're in bed before I get home?"

Getting reassurance from Imani, Naomi praises the heavens for such a considerate babysitter. Emotionally exhausted, Naomi gets up from her desk. Seeing no one in the hallway, she grabs the small pink flashlight she keeps in her purse. Are you really going to do this? she asks herself.

Feeling, with every fiber of her being, that she is the only person who will make Michelle's disappearance a number one priority, Naomi steels her resolve with a deep breath and heads down the hallway.

Michelle's doorway is covered with a big yellow X emblazoned with the words CAUTION: DO NOT ENTER. POLICE CRIME SCENE.

Her heart in her throat, Naomi quickly glances up and down the hallway again. Still empty. She tries the door handle and is surprised to find it's unlocked. In one swift motion, Naomi opens the door and ducks through the bottom of the X.

The room looks and feels even more disturbed than it did when Andre flipped on the light that morning. The thought of strangers poking around in her friend's office is making

Naomi's skin crawl. "Don't touch anything," she whispers to herself in a shaky voice. Turning on her flashlight, she begins to look around.

No one knows Michelle as well as I do, she thinks. If there's a clue in this room, I'll spot it. Naomi trains her flashlight on the bookshelf to the right of Michelle's desk and begins scanning the shelves from right to left. Seeing nothing, she moves behind Michelle's desk, bumping Michelle's chair and moving it slightly. Damn. Have to be more careful. The bottom right drawer is slightly open. Taking a deep breath, she pulls the drawer completely open to find one of Michelle's favorite earrings on top of an unmarked large manila envelope. She suspects that the investigators would have spotted this as easily as she had but is glad to see that it was left behind. Maybe they are planning to go through Michelle's files tomorrow; her laptop hasn't been seized yet either, Naomi thinks, eyeing the laptop on the left side of Michelle's desk, moved from its usual spot in the center but not taken. Naomi wastes no time grabbing the emerald green earring in one hand and the envelope in the other. Clues, she thinks.

Taking care to return the drawer and the chair to their original positions, Naomi scans the room once more. Better not push my luck. Time to get out of here, she prompts herself. She does her best to use the sleeve of her blouse to wipe off anything she might have touched.

She listens carefully through the closed door for any noises in the hall. Hearing nothing, she quietly opens Michelle's door and carefully maneuvers herself around the tape, making sure no one appears in the hallway. Holding the envelope and earring close to her chest, she rushes back down the hallway toward her office, closing the door behind her once she's safely inside.

CHAPTER 4

Now safely in her office, Naomi drops the envelope and earring inside her briefcase and returns the pink flashlight to her purse. The heartbeat in her head is so loud it's drowning out her thoughts. Now is not the time to find out the contents of the envelope. I will open it once I'm home, she thinks.

Making that her final decision, she does her best to catch up on some work that got pushed to the back burner because of the day's distractions. She stares at her computer screen for what seems like hours before realizing her efforts are futile. She is incapable of concentrating on anything else besides Michelle's disappearance.

Calling it a day, she gathers up her purse, lunch case, and briefcase. On her way out, she glances toward the caution tape covering Michelle's door and gets a chill. She is consumed by thoughts of what the envelope she found in Michelle's office might contain and is startled when the elevator door opens and Andre is inside. She takes a step back and quickly smiles to cover her surprise.

He smiles back.

"Just making my rounds through the building and I noticed your car was still in the parking lot. I was definitely coming with the intention of sending you home, but from the looks of it, you are already on your way out."

"I just needed to finish up a few things before calling it quits for the day. It was hard to be productive today with all the distractions." Sounds credible enough, she thinks.

Making it to the lobby, they exit the elevator together. Passing the security desk, Andre keeps up with her pace. One eyebrow raised, Naomi looks at him but keeps walking toward the glass doors.

"Just walking you to your car, if you don't mind."

Nodding her approval, they walk out together.

Nearing her car, Naomi gives Andre a quick "thanks" over her shoulder and unlocks the driver's side with her key fob. She is about to open her door when she realizes that Andre is still behind her. In fact, he's so close she can almost feel him.

Turning to face him, she asks, "What are you doing?"

"Come on, Naomi. You know I've had a thing for you for the last two years since I've been working here. All the flirting we do; there's no way you could be clueless." He takes his hand and caresses her face.

Looking into his eyes, she says, "Flirting with you on a daily basis is one thing, accepting your advances is another. I think we should just stick to . . ."

Before she can finish, he kisses her deeply, pinning her against the car. Grabbing her waist, he deepens the kiss. Taken completely off guard, she gives in to him, losing herself for about thirty seconds. He begins to grab at her blouse, never losing eye contact, and she suddenly comes to her senses. She turns her head to break the kiss and pushes his chest off of hers. Allowing her to break the embrace, Andre just stands there waiting for Naomi to say something.

Looking him up and down, she is briefly tempted. James certainly has some things to explain, but two wrongs don't make a right. She has far too much at home to lose. She reaches out to touch Andre's chest.

Her raspy voice manages to say, "We are just friends, Andre."

With disappointment in his eyes, he turns around and starts walking back toward the building, shaking his head.

Leaning back on her car, her legs quiver. God, he almost had me, she thinks. She closes her eyes and waits for the excitement that his advances created to subside. She opens them a few moments later, opens her door, throws her belongings onto the passenger seat, and gets in. Feeling her own wetness between her legs, she starts the car and heads home for the night, in a state of curiosity.

Imani is curled up on the couch watching something on TV when Naomi gets home. As instructed, the kids are already in bed.

"Imani, I hope it wasn't too much trouble asking you to stay a little bit later tonight. I know you have some classes tomorrow."

"No problem, Mrs. T! I love those two little ones upstairs. I never have a problem with spending any extra moments I can get." She smiles sweetly.

Naomi takes a hundred-dollar bill from her wallet and hands it to Imani.

"Thank you so much, sweetheart. Do you need me to drive you down the street?"

"No, it's only a few houses down. I'm sure I can manage," she says, bouncing up off the couch and putting the bill in her front pocket.

"Well, at least let me walk you to the door."

At the door, Imani turns around to face Naomi, looking unsure about something. Then she hugs Naomi goodbye. Accepting the young girl's embrace, Naomi smiles.

"Text me once you make it home so I know you made it safe." It's an exchange they've shared a hundred times.

"Sure thing." Imani steps off the porch onto the walkway, never turning around again.

Naomi closes the door once Imani reaches the main sidewalk. Locking the door, she heads back to the kitchen, where she placed her belongings. Just seeing the note on the fridge, she walks up to it.

Hanging out with the guys for a little bit, love. I'll see you later. Love you, Jay.

Grateful to be in complete seclusion, she crumples the note and opens her briefcase. Looking around the room as if someone could be watching her, she takes the manila envelope out first then searches for the earring, which has become sand-wiched between piles of papers.

She is shocked when she opens the envelope. Naomi can't believe her eyes as she shuffles through graphic images of Jason and Michelle making love in what appears to be a cheap hotel. Looking for a clue as to where the pictures may have come from, she starts flipping them over. On the back of one of the photos, written in black marker, she reads, FOR YOU, MR. GREELEY, DETECTIVE P.

Dropping the photos on the island, Naomi pours herself a healthy glass of chardonnay. The wheels in her head start turning. So, Norman hired a private detective to catch Michelle cheating, she thinks. Who knew he cared at all.

Pacing the kitchen with her wine glass in her hand, she pauses briefly to look at the earring, remembering that Michelle was wearing those exact earrings the last time she saw her. But where is she? Naomi's pacing has taken her in a full circle around the marble-topped island as scenario after scenario plays in her mind of what could have happened to her dear friend.

She must find out more, but where can she look? The spare car key! Michelle gave her one in case she ever locked her keys inside. But Naomi had overheard the investigators say that Michelle's car wasn't in the company parking garage or parking lot.

Just then a light bulb went off in her head. Norman has the car, she thinks. Unless, that is, the police have already seized it as evidence. With this newfound epiphany, Naomi knows she has to find out if Michelle's car is at home in her garage. Along with these photos, that will be enough damning evidence to make the police take a long, hard look at Norman Greeley.

Just then, she hears the garage door of her own home lifting and begins scrambling to put the photographs and now the earring inside the manila envelope. She stuffs the envelope back into her briefcase securely, just as her drunken husband floats around the corner into the kitchen.

Eyes glossy, he is grinning from ear to ear. "I was hoping you were still up."

Glancing down at her watch, she's surprised to see it's one in the morning.

CHAPTER 5

Walking with a swagger toward his wife, James leans down to kiss Naomi. He immediately sweeps her into an embrace as he deepens the kiss, pulling her purple blouse from her black slacks. She moans as James bites her lip tenderly.

With Naomi up against the island, James breaks their lips and starts unbuttoning her blouse, never losing eye contact. His eyes are intense; his smile is knowing.

Now shirtless, Naomi begins to untuck the polo shirt covering James' powerful upper body. With a growing urgency, James grabs his shirt's bottom hem and pulls it over his head and tosses it onto the floor. In unison, they reach for each other's pants and start to undress each other completely.

Pulling her pants to the floor, James smiles at the sight of Naomi's pink lace boyshorts. He drops to his knees, moving closer to her. Looking up at her as she looks down at him, he places his hands on the top of her underpants and pulls them down slowly until they are at her feet.

Looking at an expertly waxed hairless jewel, he grabs her foot and gently raises it until it's resting on top of the marble island. Then he begins to devour her hidden treasure below.

Gripping the counter in ecstasy, Naomi quietly moans, mindful that there are two children asleep upstairs. James reaches ever deeper with his tongue, hungry for her sweetness. Naomi can no longer hold back her cries.

"That's right, James. Eat that pussy."

James moans in response.

"Fuck. I'm about to cum all over your face."

Naomi's knees weaken. Catching her before she falls onto the ivory tile, James doesn't miss a beat. As soon as Naomi's back touches the cool floor, she cums into James' mouth, with a cry of pleasure that is sure to wake the children upstairs. But in a daze, Naomi doesn't care about that now.

Looking up at her lover and husband, she watches as he pulls down his pants and releases his manhood. Grabbing himself in delight, he strokes himself a few times. Then he locks eyes with the woman who adores him.

Widening her legs to get closer to her warmest place, he inserts himself inside with just a small amount of force, making her inhale in pleasure. They immediately begin their rhythm. Panting and groaning, their speed increases slightly.

James pulls one of her breasts from her black bra and begins to suck tenderly on her rock-hard nipple.

With her eyes closed tight, Naomi can't help but moan as he deepens the stroke. Feeling herself about to climax for the second time, Naomi grabs her crumpled shirt from the floor and covers her mouth with it. She can tell by James' quickening pace that his own climax is approaching. Turned on by the new tempo, Naomi is on her way to her third climax when James explodes inside her with a low growl.

Overcome with pleasure and fatigue, Naomi bursts into laughter. "A growl! Really, James?"

"Hush, woman. Let's go upstairs and make sure you didn't wake up our kids with all that screaming. They probably think you're dead down here."

Slapping the top of his head. "Asshole."

James gets up from the floor first, and then turns around to help his wife.

Their legs are quivering, and they both giggle at their unsteadiness.

Finding her lace panties, Naomi steps each foot inside a leg opening. She turns back around to find James staring at her in amusement. Tilting her head, with one hand on her hip, she smiles.

"See something you like?"

"Maybe I do."

Putting out his hand for her to grab, he says sleepily, "Come on crazy lady. Let's go check on the kids." Taking her hand in his, they head toward the stairs, holding hands all the way to the top.

Breaking hands, they both head toward the room where the kids usually sleep together to help ward off imaginary monsters in the dark. James peers inside the cracked door and sees two small bodies, completely covered with blankets up to their heads. His son is on his back in one of the twin beds; his daughter is on her stomach in the other. He smiles.

Before he can say anything, the door widens with a creak. Naomi's head peeks around James' muscular arm, and she smiles at the same sight.

Heading to their master suite, hand in hand, James pushes the door open and Naomi jumps into bed wearing just her panties. A now slothful James takes the items from his jeans pockets—cellphone, keys, wallet, a few random receipts—and places everything on his nightstand, making sure to put his phone on the charger. Looking at a now resting Naomi, he smiles. Removing his jeans, he climbs into bed with her, sighing as his head hits the pillow. James falls asleep quickly.

Hearing the beginning of his snores, Naomi nestles up against the love of her life and begins to drift off into her own dream world. But after fifteen to twenty minutes, a constant buzzing interrupts her sleep. Too tired to care, she squeezes her eyes closed, willing herself to sleep against the noise. But the miserable noise isn't stopping, and James isn't moving. Frustrated, Naomi leans over her husband's body and finds the source of her misery. His phone buzzes a final time, displaying a name across the screen: *Nicole*.

Dropping back onto her side of the bed, Naomi stares at the ceiling. What the fuck?

Her mind and heart unsettled, Naomi's eyes begin to get heavy, exhausted from the day's events. She blinks slowly as a few tears fall, before she drifts into dreamland with uncertainty in her heart.

Naomi is running down the middle of her street in pitch-blackness. Not one porch light is lit. Picking up her pace, she sprints faster, pushing herself harder, determined to get away from whomever or whatever is dogging her in the darkness.

No matter how fast she runs, Naomi never leaves her street. The scenery never changes. She steals a look behind her as she runs wildly for any safety that might lie ahead. From the corner of her eye, she spots an object on the ground ahead of her. Running closer to it, she sees it's a boot that looks identical to a pair that Michelle owns, and she bends down in confusion to grab the boot. With her fingertips barely touching the shoe, the scenery suddenly shifts. No longer reaching out for the shoe, she is now walking through the hallway in her office building, headed in the direction of her office.

Quickening her steps, feeling an urgent need to reach safety, she is almost to her door. Passing Michelle's office, she hears a scream from the other side of the door. She grabs the bronze doorknob but instead of Michelle's office, the door opens into Naomi's office where she is facing her desk. Before she turns around, she knows he is behind her. She can feel his breath. A warm feeling washes over her, and she melts once he begins to nibble her ear. Naomi looks down and notices that she is wearing a gray wrap-around dress with nothing underneath. Her feet are bare. The man's hand reaches around her to grab her right breast. She wants to tell him to stop but all she can do is groan with pleasure. At the sound of her pleasure, he exposes her breasts, then turns her to face him. With desire in his eyes, he sucks each nipple tenderly, forcing another cry from her mouth.

Grabbing her hair, he pulls her head back to expose a neck that he so eagerly begins to devour. Breathing heavier, Naomi moans with delight and anticipation of what is to come. With a grin on his face, he lets go of her hair and takes a step back. Without hesitation, Naomi drops to her knees, undoes the zipper of his pants, and takes him inside her warm, inviting mouth. Now he is the one moaning with pleasure, as she moves her head back and forth.

Quickening her pace, he grabs a fist full of her curly hair, guiding her to the base of his throbbing manhood. He matches her rhythm as his head tilts back, and she allows him to go deeper down her throat. No longer able to take the pleasure of her mouth, he pulls her to her feet and pushes her against her desk, knocking a few things to the floor. Moving closer between her legs, their lips touch with intensely magnetic heat. Pulling the string holding her dress together, he breaks their lips to look down at her body. He grins.

"I told you I would have you one day."

His hands begin to caress her body, starting at her neck, down to her breasts. He pauses there for a moment to play with each nipple, and then lowers his mouth to suck each one. She exhales.

Lifting his head, his hands continue to move down her body. She begins to quiver. His hands trace the outline of every inch of her upper body, his brown eyes trailing as his hands progress until he reaches her hips. Excitement and anticipation of what is to come in her eyes, her legs part ever so slightly.

His eyes burn with passion; clearly, he is delighted that she is welcoming him into a place he has never ventured. Lifting her legs, he slips into the wetness he created with an exhale of his own. He is stroking her slowly, and with every stroke, a murmur escapes her lips. As their excitement builds, he quickens his pace. Grabbing the edge of the desk, she matches his force.

Moaning and giving in to her own cries of pleasure, she is on her way to an inevitably intense climax. Her eyes close tightly. Andre is now insane with pleasure as more of the contents of her desk hit the floor. He feels the pulse of her orgasm forcing his own climax, and he pulls out and cums all over her body.

CHAPTER 6

In an instant, he vanishes, leaving her quivering, barely clothed body with a chill. Naomi's eyes open to complete solitude. Staring out her office window, with a cup of steaming Starbucks Carmel Macchiato in her favorite pink coffee mug, Naomi surveys the number of police cars in the company parking lot. The investigation has not made much progress, but it's only been a few days. Forensic analysts still control the space that was once a part of Michelle's everyday life, in hopes of finding some clue indicating her whereabouts or—in the darkest hour—her body.

It's been three days since Naomi found Michelle's emerald earring and photos of Michelle and her secret lover. But she knows she needs more. She has to find that car. The gray Audi 3 flashed in her memory. Norman has to be hiding her car somewhere, but where? Maybe all he wanted to do was talk and things got out of hand, like they usually did. He once sent Michelle on a cruise to give the bruises he put on her body time to heal.

Losing herself in her own worried thoughts, Naomi doesn't hear the first knock at her office door. The second knock is more forceful, pulling her back to reality.

"Come in, please," she grants their passage.

As soon as she sees his face, she knows the words that are about to fall from his lips. Only looking at him directly for a few seconds, Naomi finds a spot on the wall.

"Let me guess; it's time for my interview."

"Good morning, Naomi. They need you in conference room two in five minutes."

Forcing herself to look at him, Andre stands strong in his black slacks and midnight blue button-front shirt. Damn that dream from the other night. The reality of him seems twenty times better. She looks out the window again.

"Thank you for being the one to come and tell me. I can be ready in five minutes. Will you be there?"

"No. I will be in the main lobby at the front desk monitoring the cameras. More than likely I am a part of the investigation, not included in it. I just came here for you." He winks.

"You have always looked out for me, Andre. I really do love that about you." Her gaze stays fixed on the window.

Silence fills the room. Backing his way out, Andre closes the door behind him without any hesitation. Since her dream, Naomi has been effectively avoiding him, and today is the first day they actually speak. She has enough on her plate, with her best friend missing and her husband getting text messages from strange women at all hours. She can't afford to wrap herself up in intense fantasies about Andre. Not today. No, today is about answering questions in regard to Michelle and her disappearance. And Naomi is as ready as she'll ever be. She is thankful for the heads up from Andre. He really is good to her, and she quietly hopes the awkwardness created by their encounter in the parking lot starts to mend.

Clearing that distraction from her head, she moves from the window to her desk, placing down her favorite mug. She smooths out the front of her gray blouse and long navy pencil skirt, giving the room a final once over to make sure everything is in its place. She heads to the door, takes in a deep breath, and exhales before opening her office door to head down to the conference room.

Since the police had arrived, constant commotion and a buzz of people in the hallway were becoming the norm around the office. Pairs of eyes follow her down the hallway as she passes. Entering the conference room, she barely recognizes it. The long oval table surrounded completely by office chairs has vanished. In its place is a small square table with two rolling office chairs across from each other. There is one regular chair standing alone on the other side of the room.

One officer is standing by that distant chair holding a cup of coffee, waiting for the next interviewee and possibly a break in this case to enter. Another officer is sitting at the square table, dressed casually in khaki pants and a black and gray striped polo shirt, flipping through a few pages of his notes. He stands when she begins to walk up to the table, which is slightly centered in the room.

"Good morning, Mrs. Tanner. My colleague and I were just headed to your office to come get you. I am guessing the head of security informed you of our meeting time?"

"Yes, I was directed to come talk with you this morning."

"I'm Detective Ryley, Thomas Ryley. And this is Officer Stacey Ramsey." The blonde female officer smiles.

"We would like to ask you some questions about Michelle Greeley, if you are up to it today. We hear she was, I mean is, a dear friend of yours."

Nearing the table, Naomi reaches out to shake his hand and gives the detective an easy smile.

"Yes, Michelle and I have been close friends for five years. Ask me anything. I just want her to be found."

Accepting her handshake, Detective Ryley invites her to sit across from him. Following his lead, Naomi takes a seat.

"Before we begin, Mrs. Tanner, I would like to make it clear that all the interviews we conduct in this room are recorded. Are you ready to begin?"

Sitting up straight in the chair, Naomi announces, "Yes, let's get started."

Officer Ramsey presses a button on top of a digital camera mounted to a tripod, and the first question comes from Detective Ryley's mouth.

"Is your name Naomi Tanner?"

"Yes."

"Mrs. Tanner, how long have you known the missing person, Michelle Greeley?"

"Michelle and I met five years ago in this very building, and we have been best friends ever since."

"As one of her close friends, I am sure that you were aware of her personal life. Did she have any recent conflicts with anyone or had she told you about any problems she might be having at home?"

"Unfortunately, Detective, in these last few weeks she and I haven't been spending as much time together as we usually do. She had some new projects that were forcing her to work later than usual, so I may not have much information to give."

"Anything you can remember, Mrs. Tanner, would be helpful."

Sitting there for a moment, her mind begins to flash over all that she knows: there is the abuse from Norman, the affair with Jason, the phone calls in the middle of the night, and the photos neatly stuffed in her briefcase in her office. Concerned that any information she shares with them could sidetrack her own investigation, Naomi starts small.

"Well, I can honestly say that Michelle did not have the best marriage, which is usually what made her work such long hours. She and Norman have been fighting a lot recently and things have gotten physical a few times.

"Michelle often came to me with her domestic worries, but she was terrified of leaving her husband," Naomi continues. "He's a very powerful man and never has a problem flexing his strength to prove a point.

"Norman has had several, very public affairs that destroyed Michelle's confidence in her marriage. She began distancing herself even from me."

"Were you aware of any affairs that Michelle may have been having?"

There it is. Point blank. The question she has been dreading. Jason may make poor choices— like sleeping with his boss— but he's not a killer, Naomi thinks to herself. She decides to lie.

"No. But again, we have both been busy."

"Other than Mr. Greeley, is there anyone else you think we should be looking into?"

"Well, Detective, there is one other thing."

"Yes, Mrs. Tanner?"

"I received calls from Michelle in the middle of the night. It was late, and I assumed that whatever she wanted, we would talk about it the next day at work. But we never had that chance. You don't know how badly I wish I'd answered my phone that night."

"Did she leave you any messages? Do you remember exactly what time it was?"

"No, she didn't leave any messages, and it had to be two thirty, maybe three in the morning. She needed me, and I didn't answer." Naomi looks away, swallowing tears.

"Whether you know it or not, your information has been helpful. We heard a rumor that Michelle may have been having an affair with another person in the office. Can you give us any insight into who it could be? No one seems to know."

Sitting back in her chair, Naomi pretends to think. She knows very well that Michelle was having an affair with Jason Smith, but can she avoid sharing this with the police?

"Michelle did say there was something she wanted to tell me over drinks, but we never got around to it." Naomi stares off into the distance once more with worry in her heart.

Detective Ryley reaches his hand across the table.

"Thank you, Mrs. Tanner. We may have some follow-up questions in the future, but other than that, there's nothing more we need from you today."

Rising from the chair, Naomi grabs the detective's hand.

"Thank you." She forces a weak smile.

At least six sets of eyes watch her as she heads back down the hallway toward her office.

Once inside, she closes the door behind her and begins pacing. Her workload is piling up, but she knows she needs to stay focused on finding her friend. Evidence. She needs more evidence. The next step: follow Norman.

Norman's office is three floors above theirs. It's no secret how much Naomi loathes Norman for the way he treats Michelle, so getting past Norman's assistant is going to be hell. She has to spy on him some other way.

Her first thought is to follow him (secretly, of course) to figure out his normal routine—just what, exactly, is he doing while the rest of the staff is working? Normally, Naomi would flirt with Andre to get a sneak peek at the security cameras to see when Norman comes and goes, but sending Andre mixed signals at this point is clearly off the table. She's on her own for now.

CHAPTER 7

Naomi is standing in her two-person, walk-in shower, letting the water pour through her curly hair and down her back. It's five in the morning. Everyone else is still fast asleep. With only the sound of the water washing over her, Naomi allows her mind to wander.

Who can she talk to at work today about Norman's schedule without raising suspicion? No one, she thinks in defeat. Everyone who comes to mind would definitely make a connection, making the buzz among her peers louder. Damn, what will she do without Andre's help?

Just then, a figure appears to her right, pulling her from her thoughts. It's James, in all his unclothed glory. Naomi turns to welcome him, surprised by how quickly she's aroused. Her dreams aren't giving her any relief in the sex department. She needs this. Opening her arms to welcome him, they begin to kiss.

In a deep embrace, Naomi steps back under the water, bringing James along with her. Feeling the heat from the water against his chest, James makes a sound between their lips.

She breaks their kiss and leans back, her head against the blue tile, to allow James' body to feel more of the water.

Steam from the water rises all around them, and they grab each other again, kissing sensually. James runs his strong, wide hands down her back, cupping them around the fullness of her firm ass. She moans with her arms around his neck.

Breaking their embrace once again, Naomi pushes James backward onto the built-in tile seat. Reaching her hand up, she adjusts the showerhead so that the water reaches his thighs. Closing his eyes, he invites the warmth.

Stepping up to him, Naomi blocks the passage of the water, and as it flows down her back, she mounts him with an exhale.

Creating a bit faster rhythm than their usual, Naomi closes her eyes and lets her head fall back. Excited by her aggression, James leans in to suck her breasts. Feeling his warm mouth on her skin, she moans and slows down the pace just a little.

Lifting his head up with a grin, James grabs her hips, matching her rhythm and pushing her down with every roll of her hips. She looks down at him, her climax near as she moves faster. Gripping her waist tighter, he pulls her down harder.

Challenging him, she pounds harder against his every thrust. Unable to contain her inevitable scream, she grabs his shoulders and climaxes. Her legs are shaking, but, wanting more, she begins again with a slow rhythm.

Grabbing her thighs to stop her movements, James speaks for the first time that morning.

"My turn."

Allowing her to stand, James gently turns her around. Naomi places her hands on the built-in seat, and James mounts her from behind. He strokes her slowly, pausing for a second between each purposeful thrust. He is throbbing and rock-hard, and Naomi is enjoying every second as she pushes closer to her next climax. James' pace quickens, and Naomi knows this means he's nearing his own climax. He grabs her ass and goes in deeper. He takes longer strokes and grabs her hair before exploding inside her. Feeling the pulsating impact of his orgasm, she cums for the second time this morning.

Turning toward the warm water, James begins to wash himself. Propped up against the tile wall, Naomi watches patiently.

"Well, good morning," she says, as their eyes meet.

"Good morning," he smiles, reaching for the washcloth and soap.

Watching him bathe is incredibly erotic, but Naomi is spent. Embracing her husband from behind, she kisses his back, then whispers, "My turn, again."

Turning to face her, he smiles.

"OK. I'll get out of your hair." He kisses her forehead then makes his way past her. She hears the bathroom door close behind him, returning her to complete solitude.

Standing under the water, alone again, she washes her body quickly, not thinking about anything of real value. Beginning to whistle, she grabs her towel and wraps it around her, standing in a bathroom so steamy she can't see herself in the mirror. She opens the door, letting the fog roll out and spots her husband, fast asleep once again. Looking at the clock on her nightstand, she climbs back into the bed.

Forty-five more minutes won't hurt, she thinks. Nestling up closer to James, she closes her eyes.

Naomi stares blankly out her office window, holding her favorite mug, which this morning is filled with Earl Grey tea instead of coffee. She goes over the plan in her head for the fourth time. Without Andre's help at her disposal, she's had to cultivate a plan to get into Norman's office unnoticed. And the easiest way to do this is when both Norman and his assistant are nowhere near.

She remembers a previous conversation with Michelle, during which Michelle complained that Norman took two-hour lunches religiously every Tuesday without explanation. Today is Tuesday, so it's time to act, she tells herself.

Thinking back, Naomi struggles to recall the timeframe that Michelle mentioned. Was it noon to two? Or was it one to three? She can't remember but knows she has to take a chance today.

Walking to her desk, she takes her seat behind it. Flipping open her laptop, she begins her work for the day, awaiting her time to venture to the fifth floor of the building and to Norman's office —a place to which she was summoned in the not-too-distant past. She recalls their conversation as vividly as if it just happened yesterday.

Norman was sitting behind his desk in a gray pinstriped, Giorgio Armani suit. His dress shirt was plum-colored. He didn't look up to acknowledge her until his door had completely closed behind her.

He looked up from his newspaper, folded it, and placed it on his desk with a sneer.

"I called you into my office this morning to tell you to end your friendship with my wife. She doesn't need a woman like you putting ideas in her head."

Knowing exactly why "Lord Greeley" had summoned her, Naomi couldn't suppress the snicker that fell from her lips.

Surprised because he had given her his best "try me if you dare" look, he leaned forward in his chair.

"This is not a joke. End your friendship or lose your job today, Mrs. Tanner."

Her initial look of shock quickly flashed to rage. With anger in her voice, she spoke.

"On what grounds? I have done nothing but great things at this company. The quality of my work is not in jeopardy. And as for your request, you can shove it up your ass."

Not giving him another chance to speak, she exited the room immediately, only to be greeted by his firm-breasted, bleached-blonde secretary, Kimberley McCormick, who also knew the reason for the visit.

"Good morning, Mrs. Tanner. I shouldn't expect you will be having a return visit?"

Ignoring her, Naomi stormed past her desk toward the elevators.

Coming back to the present, she begins absentmindedly tapping the keys in front of her. She's on autopilot now and simply going through the motions until it's time to visit Norman's office.

Because she can't remember exactly when he's supposed to be gone, she plans for the possibility of making two trips to the fifth floor if needed.

Looking down at the clock on her laptop, she sees it's 12:15 p.m.

Rising from her desk, she reaches into her purse and grabs the pair of latex gloves she picked up from the store yesterday. Grabbing her mini pink flashlight and phone, she walks to her office door and opens it.

A few people walk by, too deep in conversation about whatever exciting drama today's interview investigations have generated to look in Naomi's direction. Perfect, she thinks. The focus of her peers has shifted since nothing, as far as they could tell, came of her interview with the police.

She waits until the group reaches the elevators and steps inside before she heads down the hallway and, with one quick glance over her shoulder to make sure no one's watching, ducks into the stairwell. Glad that she remembered to wear comfortable, Tory Burch flats, Naomi moves quickly up the stairwell to the fifth floor door.

Pausing to look through the door's small square window before opening the door, she waits until two people pass by on their way to the elevators. Hearing the familiar "ding" as the elevator doors open, Naomi counts to three before pulling the stairwell door open and heading to the left, toward Norman's office.

Norman's assistant Kimberley is still sitting at her desk, filing her nails, when Norman suddenly appears in his office doorway.

Spotting a women's restroom, Naomi quickly ducks inside and hides in a stall until her watch says 12:35.

Walking once again toward Norman's office, she can see that his door is now closed but Kimberley remains at her desk talking with another secretary. Naomi slows her pace and tries to overhear what the women are saying.

"Well, if today is like every other Tuesday, Mr. Greeley will be gone for at least two hours, maybe even a little longer. Going out to lunch sounds perfect!"

Yes! One small victory! Naomi thinks as she walks swiftly past the office door. Realizing the hallway she is heading down is a dead end, Naomi bends down and pretends to make an adjustment to her shoe. Glancing around, she is glad to find that no one has noticed her.

Naomi watches as Kimberley and her friend grab their purses and head in the direction of the elevators.

Praying that the outer office door is unlocked, Naomi makes her way toward Kimberley's desk and steps inside the outer office unnoticed. With her back against an inside wall, she waits as she hears more people seemingly leaving for lunch. Once the fifth floor falls silent, Naomi moves from the wall and tries the door to Norman's office. This is her lucky day. Turning the handle, she is granted access.

Naomi looks over the room and realizes that, in the afternoon sunlight, there is no need for the flashlight hidden in her closed hand. Geesh. She is letting this detective thing cloud her thinking! She scans the room, which looks exactly as it did the last time she was here. Not one thing out of place. Walking up to his desk, she begins to look at the contents in front of her.

Just then, Naomi hears voices approaching the door. Panicking, she climbs under Norman's mahogany desk. The door swings open and in walks Kimberley, still talking.

"I promised I would take these letters on Mr. Greeley's desk to the mailroom, then it's sushi for lunch, Christina. I'm starving."

With Kimberley's feet right in front of her, Naomi tries not to breathe. Then a sparkle catches Naomi's eye. It shimmers green. Naomi's eyes widen. She can hear Kimberley grab the letters and exit the room, still in conversation with her friend. Waiting until she hears the door close behind Kimberley, Naomi crawls toward the shiny green object.

Under the small glass end table against the wall is an emerald green earring that matches the one Naomi retrieved from Michelle's office days before. Grabbing the earring in her fingers, Naomi sits up and holds the earring up to the sunlight for a closer look. Damn, it matches perfectly. Getting to her feet, she continues to examine the room.

She walks back over to his desk and, spotting the calendar on which he's noted multiple upcoming events, Naomi pulls out her phone and takes a picture. Satisfied with her results, she slips her phone and the earring into her pocket and exits Norman's office.

Moving quickly, she slips through the outer office where Kimberley's desk sits and into the main hallway, grateful to find herself alone. She makes her way casually toward the stairwell.

Once inside the stairwell, she exhales, wondering if somehow she'd been holding her breath the entire time she was on the fifth floor. Going down the stairs is much easier than going up had been, and as she safely reaches the inside of her office, she pulls the flashlight from her pocket and drops it into her purse along with the rubber gloves.

Walking over to her desk, she rubs the emerald earring between her fingers and looks at the image saved on her phone to make sure it's clear enough to see all the details she needs for her next steps. More clues, proving that Norman is involved in the disappearance of his wife, she thinks.

The sudden knock at her office door makes her jump. Placing the earring in the top drawer of her desk, she answers, "Come in."

The look on Andre's face is serious. He doesn't speak until he closes her door completely behind him.

"Care to share why you were on the fifth floor?"

Naomi's eyes widen.

"I'm sure I have no idea what you're talking about. I've been in my office since this morning."

"Hmm. Well, camera footage shows a woman who looks like you entering and exiting the stairwell in the last hour," Andre replies with a hint of sarcasm.

Looking down at the clock on her laptop, she notes that it's 1:45 p.m.

"Luckily, the person on camera never looks up, and the video images aren't clear enough *for my security team* to identify any member of the staff, so *we* decided it wasn't worth handing over to the police."

And with that, Andre turns and leaves her office before she gets a chance to lie for the second time.

Sliding her laptop to the side, Naomi places her head on her desk. Even though Andre is keeping his distance, his visit this afternoon reminds Naomi that he is still watching.

CHAPTER 8

Running along the trail in Clinton River Park like she does every morning before the rest of the world is awake, a local woman tugs at her dog, Fefe, who normally isn't so easily distracted. Removing one earbud, she yells at her dog to keep up when the overwhelming odor sends her jogging in the same direction as her German shepherd.

The dog is near a bush, barking and running around in circles. The woman peers behind the bush and sees what appears to be the hand of a female, buried beneath some dirt and mulch. She moves in closer and sees a gold bracelet, and more of the woman's shallowly buried features come into view.

Backing away in shock, she presses a button on the headset dangling around her neck.

"Call 911."

Then, trying her best to stay calm, she utters the words, "I'm calling to report a body."

Naomi is standing in her kitchen, drinking her coffee while two snickering little ones eat their Cheerios for breakfast. The morning news is about to begin.

"Good morning, Detroit. Let's start with a forecast for this wonderful Saturday," announces the anchorwoman.

As the weather report begins, Naomi is thankful for the sunny forecast. Great! I'll have a picnic with the kids at the park. We'll make a day of it, she thinks.

"We do have some breaking news to report this morning. It seems a woman's body has been found at Clinton River Park. The woman has not yet been identified, but early reports indicate that we may be looking at a homicide. Reporter Richard Williams is live at the scene."

Paralyzed, Naomi drops her mug and it shatters on the floor as she stares in frozen disbelief at the small television on the kitchen counter. She's no longer hearing the words the reporter is speaking. In the pit of her stomach she knows it's Michelle.

The sound of the mug breaking startles the little ones, and James surfaces in the kitchen doorway. Spotting the broken mug and Naomi's blank stare, James crosses the kitchen, unconcerned that pieces of the broken mug are crunching under his feet.

"Naomi."

Tears burst from her eyes as her body slumps, on her way to the white tile floor. Catching her before she hits the floor, James speaks again.

"Naomi, what's going on?"

"Mmm-Michelle has been missing, and I think someone just found her body this morning," Naomi stutters as the tears fall.

"What? Why am I just finding out about this?"

"You've been busy, and I haven't been able to talk about it with anyone. I just prayed the police would find her before anything bad happened."

Or that I would find her, Naomi thinks.

"Mommy, what's wrong? Why are you crying? Did you get a boo-boo?" asks Daniel from his perch beside the kitchen island.

Through painstaking tears, Naomi smiles. "No, Daniel. Mommy didn't get a boo-boo. She is just worried about Aunt Michelle right now."

"Is Aunt Michelle on the news?"

"Mommy's not sure, but I'm definitely going to find out," Naomi says with newfound determination.

Turning back to James, she meets the concern in his eyes.

"What exactly do you plan on doing, Naomi? This isn't one of your hobbies." Looking over at the children, James chooses his words wisely. Remembering the childhood friend Naomi lost, his brow visibly strains with concern.

He grabs Naomi's hands and speaks calmly.

"Please let the police handle this. There could be more danger involved than either of us are aware of, and I don't want to be worried about you. You know the pre-season is about to begin."

Fully aware of her husband's upcoming schedule, she says reassuringly, "Of course, I will let the police handle it. Don't worry my love."

Getting to her feet and trying to seem OK for everyone's sake, she wipes her eyes. But she senses that James can see right through her.

"I mean it. Promise me that you won't go looking into this yourself. It may not be Michelle after all and she's just on another Norman-imposed vacation while her bruises heal."

Turning around to face the sink instead of her husband, she remembers why she said nothing about the disappearance. She pushes down the emptiness in her heart.

In the happiest voice she can muster, Naomi says, "Of course! I'm sure you're right."

"Promise me, Naomi."

"Promise, James," she lies. Little does he know, she already is involved.

Her thoughts shift to the picture she took of Norman's schedule. She will know his movements from next Monday through the following Tuesday. Naomi is glad to have more than a week's worth of his schedule, as she has yet to think about any form of surveillance. With James leaving town tonight and not coming back until Friday, this is the perfect time to begin following Norman. Especially now that it appears he's just become a murderer. The hatred grows in her heart. Maybe she will ask Imani to stay later, possibly overnight a few nights next week. They have a guest room, and that will make it easier for Naomi to come and go at any time. Naomi makes a mental note to reach out to Imani's parents to make sure it will not be a problem. Naomi turns to face her husband, greeting him with a smile.

"Don't worry, honey. I won't get into any trouble while you're gone." She walks over to the two tiny humans that mean the world to her and bends down in front of them.

"See, Daniel, Mommy feels better. But you know what would make Mommy feel the happiest?"

The concern in his eyes changes to delight. "What, Mommy?"

"Daniel and Serena kisses!"

Naomi wraps her arms around them both and showers them with kisses all over their faces, heads, shoulders, and necks. Both of them giggle with excitement. Satisfied that she has calmed her family, she turns to James once more.

"I was thinking of taking the kids on a picnic. Would you care to join us before you leave tonight?"

"Awe, babe. I already promised a few guys that I would meet up with them for some practice drills and evening drinks. I was going to leave for the airport from there."

Somehow, Naomi knew this would be his response. She turns away and forces herself to swallow her grief and disappointment for the sake of the children.

Coming up behind her, James grabs both of Naomi's shoulders and squeezes.

"Please don't be upset with me. I will make it up to you guys as soon as I get back. I promise."

Turning to face him, she stands on her toes to catch his bottom lip with a kiss.

"It had better be spectacular. The kids and I miss being a family with you, but I also understand that football is a big part of all of our lives. There will be other invitations that you had better not miss out on." And with that, she smiles to show her forgiveness.

Grabbing the two empty cereal bowls and spoons, she speaks. "Daniel, take your sister in the living room and watch some *Daniel Tiger's Neighborhood* while Mommy cleans up in here."

"Come on, Serena. I want to watch Daniel Tiger." Getting up from the seat, Daniel extends his hand to his sister.

Accepting her brother's invitation, Serena slides off the seat and takes his hand. They walk to the living room hand in hand.

Watching the two of them, the tightness in Naomi's chest eases slightly. With dishes in her hand, Naomi turns around to see an awaiting James. She can tell he's looking for any signs of defiance.

"I'm fine, James. Like you said, it's probably not Michelle and I'm overreacting."

"I know that you are just saying this, so I will get out of your hair. But I mean it, Naomi."

Knowing that her plans are already in motion, she brushes past him to get to the sink. There are too many feelings and emotions to hide from the scrutiny of his eyes. Washing out the bowls, she speaks, barely masking the aggravation in her voice.

"James, I said I would leave things alone. What more would you like me to say?"

Coming up close behind her, he bends down to her ear and whispers. "I'd like you to mean it."

The authority in his tone sends a little chill down her back. She closes her eyes.

"I am sure the police will be able to handle this. We still don't even know it's her. Maybe she really is on vacation." She is hoping with all of her heart that this is the case, but in her core, she knows the truth. She felt the loss instantly. She has to find out what happened.

Bringing Naomi from her thoughts, James speaks.

"I love you. I just don't want to see you in harm's way. I need to know you're safe while I'm away."

Turning around from the sink, she wraps her arms around his neck and crosses her fingers. She kisses him deeply, not wanting to say another word. Not wanting to tell another lie. The truth is, she loves James more than anything, but her best friend has possibly been murdered. He can't possibly believe that she's just going to sit around and not get some answers; that has never been her. At least, not since losing Briana so long ago.

James accepts her kiss of peace, opening his mouth to allow her tongue inside. She moans before breaking their connection.

"You better stop before you start something in this kitchen."

"Maybe that's what I'm trying to do." He gives his cutest smile.

Naomi can do nothing but return the same. Thinking about his hardness, she bites her bottom lip. Immediately, she turns back around to the sink, with one spoon still left to wash.

"Didn't you say you were on your way out the door?"

Looking over at his bag by the kitchen doorway, he speaks in a low growl, pushing his manhood into her lower back.

"I'm sure I could spare five minutes."

Naomi smiles. "Not today you can't. Our two mini-mes are too close for that."

"Touché." He steps away from her.

Walking toward his bag, he speaks. "You are definitely in some trouble once I get back."

"I'm counting on it."

He turns and their eyes meet. Reaching down, he grabs the handle of his bag.

"I'll see you later, my love." And just like that, he heads out the door.

Now that she thinks about it, maybe it's not such a bad idea that James won't be joining them at the park today. It will give her more time to look over the clues she's collected and more time to figure out her next steps. She needs to point the police toward Norman without giving herself away.

CHAPTER 9

Loving the heat on her skin, Naomi has eyed the perfect spot in the park. A safe enough distance to still have full view of the playground but secluded enough so that other parents can't see the things in her possession, plus a large tree and bush provide some shade for the picnic table. Gripping one tiny hand in each of hers, she presses forward toward the chosen spot.

Their excitement clear to anyone watching, Daniel and Serena skip wildly on each side of her. All she can do is smile, relishing in the appreciation that Imani was able to join her for today's outing. Someone has to keep an eye on the children while Naomi shifts her focus to her secret mission.

Naomi looks over her shoulder to find Imani trailing behind them, pulling the cooler filled with ham and cheese, turkey and cheese, and chicken salad sandwiches; juice for the little people; Dr. Pepper for Imani; Gatorade for Naomi; and enough water for each of them to have at least two bottles a piece. On her left shoulder Imani carries Naomi's briefcase— its presence Naomi casually chalked up to needing to catch up on a few things for work. Imani's face had wrinkled at the mention of the briefcase coming along on their special outing, but Naomi's well-rehearsed excuse did the trick.

Releasing the two frenzied hands that were getting hard to hold, Naomi continues her walk to the designated spot as Daniel and Serena run toward the wooden and plastic jungle gyms, Imani still en route. Reaching the picnic table, Naomi waits for Imani, taking a seat to face the park and the approaching young woman.

"Mrs. T, I don't know why you would want to work on a beautiful day like this. You need to relax more. Sometimes it's OK to enjoy the roses."

Naomi smiles. "Just sorting through some things to get ready for next week. That doesn't mean that Daniel and Serena should suffer on this amazing day. I certainly didn't want to be trapped in an office working. Some fresh air is what we all need."

Appearing satisfied with Naomi's response, Imani hands the strap of the briefcase to Naomi and parks the cooler at the end of the picnic table.

Watching Imani walk toward the playground, Naomi reaches for the snap lock on her briefcase. She quickly glances up to see if anyone is looking in her direction. No eyes meet hers. Excellent, she thinks.

First, she pulls out the envelope containing the photos. Michelle's infidelity flashes across her mind. Next, she pulls out her phone to view the recorded schedule.

She opens the envelope first and turns it upside down so that the emerald earring drops coldly into her warm hand. She then retrieves her last and most important clue. Reaching a little further into her briefcase, her fingers rub across the jewel and her friend's face glows in the back of her mind. She slowly pulls out the matching emerald earring that she found in Norman's office. Bringing her hand closer to her face, she gently rubs the earring against her cheek, deep in thought.

This has to mean something. What happened? Did they argue about her affair and things went too far? Did Michelle purposely drop her earrings to leave a trail? Why is he still walking free, living his life, while her friend is missing and possibly dead?

She knows she has to find a way to shine a spotlight on him, on a case that currently has no suspects. People are still being interviewed. With any hope, someone else saw something. But for now, she is on a mission to find the truth. Stuck in her thoughts, she mindlessly eyes the picture of his calendar and then forces herself to engage.

Monday:

10:30 a.m. meeting with Mr. Evans

12:30 p.m. lunch with Amanda

Tuesday:

2:15 p.m. drinks with Pedro

6:30 p.m. dinner with Stephanie

8:30 p.m. Club Phyno

Clearly, Norman isn't even trying to hide the fact that he entertains other women. But who is Pedro? Is he the one who sent the photos to Norman?

Naomi craves the answers to her questions. They would only lead her closer to the truth. She reread his Monday schedule, committing it to memory.

On Monday, she won't take her BMW to work because that midnight blue beauty screams for attention. Instead, the black Audi i35 seems like the perfect fit. She only drives her second car to work a few times a month, just to get some usage.

She will go into work just a little bit earlier than usual so that she can park in the parking garage unnoticed, as avoiding detection is a vital component of her plan. Security patrols the parking garage and parking lot twice an hour. If it's the usual staff riding around in their golf cart, it's more like once an hour, she thinks, grateful for their lack in diligence.

Sitting in the park, lost in her thoughts, Naomi is startled by a rustle in the bushes behind her. Gripping an earring in each fist, she turns slowly to see what or who has caught her red handed. Expecting to see eyes looking back at her, Naomi sees nothing. Squinting, she tries to block out the sun with her other hand to get a better view.

Is someone standing in the shadows? No, it couldn't be. She has just become increasingly paranoid in the last week. Putting the earrings in one hand, she grabs the envelope and quickly stuffs everything back into her briefcase, all the while looking and listening for the slightest movement nearby.

I'm definitely losing it a little bit. Who would have reason to stalk me? Naomi lets out an airy laugh to calm her nerves. The sight of him quickly approaching puts an instant smile on her face.

"Mommy, Mommy, Mommy!" Daniel is yelling from the small hill leading to the picnic table. He is running as fast as his little legs will go.

"Slow down, Daniel."

He reaches the table out of breath. "May I have a juice please, Mommy?"

"Yes, Daniel. You are welcome to a juice. We will be having lunch in about thirty minutes. Make sure you tell Imani."

Grabbing a tiny bottle of juice, Daniel turns to run back to the playground.

"Wait one minute, mister."

Daniel turns to face his mother.

"Drink that juice at this table, not on the playground."

With sad eyes that could stop a heart, Daniel pleads, "Please, Mommy."

"You know the rules, Daniel."

Dragging his feet, only a few steps from his starting point, Daniel climbs onto the picnic table bench.

"Once you have finished your juice, then you can go back to playing."

"Yes, ma'am."

There is a pause, as though Daniel has more to say.

Raising her left eyebrow, Naomi dares him.

"Mommy, are you going to play with Serena and me?"

She looks down at her gray polo shirt, darkly stained jeans, and her favorite walking sneakers. Perfect park wardrobe.

"As soon as you finish your juice, it's a deal," she says, giving Daniel the biggest smile.

Only halfway done with the contents in his hand, Daniel drinks just a little faster.

Going over her plans in her head for the thirtieth time, a satisfying smirk crosses her lips. She snaps the lock on her briefcase and places it between the cooler and bench leg as Daniel finishes the last of his juice. The park is fairly empty today—only a few moms and nannies out in the sun with children. That's one of the things she loves about this park—mild to light traffic. Not to mention, the unobstructed view of the playground from every picnic table.

Grabbing the empty juice container in one hand and Daniel's hand in the other, Naomi heads for the nearest trash can. Before they can get halfway there, Serena and Imani appear at the top of the hill.

"We want juice too, Mommy," Serena squeals.

Where one leads, the other always follows, Naomi thinks with a smile.

"Well, we might as well have lunch. Who wants sandwiches?"

Releasing Daniel's hand, Naomi reaches the table first and bends down to open the cooler.

"To the table you two. What kind of sandwiches do you want?"

"Ham and cheese, please," Daniel recites.

"Ham and cheese, please," mimics Serena.

Pulling one sandwich out of its bag, Naomi breaks it in half.

Grabbing the half sandwiches, both children's eyes light up in anticipation.

Too bad everyone can't be pleased so easily, Naomi thinks, finally sitting at the picnic table to watch her little people ravenously devour their sandwiches.

CHAPTER 10

She stands in a completely still kitchen with her first cup of coffee, staring out her kitchen window into the darkness of early morning. With the investigation still ongoing, Naomi wonders if the woman in the park has been identified. The waiting is almost too much to bear.

The day has not quite begun, and Naomi appreciates the silence and solitude, if only for a few moments before her plans for the day begin. She has gone over today's plan so many times in her head that sleeping was next to impossible last night. Every move has to be calculated. There is no getting caught.

Her mind flashes to Andre's remarks about her last attempt at being discreet.

Instinctively, she walks over to the keys for her Audi, reminding herself that this is the vehicle she has chosen for the week. She rubs her fingers over the plastic fob, reminding herself to park in the garage where she is least likely to draw attention, instead of outside in the parking lot.

This time will be different. She is better prepared for the security cameras and knows where there's a blind spot to park in. In fact, in her earlier years of illustrious spontaneity, she and James had taken advantage of that very same spot when he occasionally had to drive her to work.

Immediately, her smile turns into a frown as she plays back the events that have made her question the security of her relationship with James. A tear escapes her eye. How can he betray her in this way so easily with no regard for the life that they have created together?

No. She has to think about the mission at hand. The news about the woman's body found in the park flashes in her mind. Finding justice for Michelle is the most important thing; she can worry about the disaster her life has become later. She lets another tear fall.

Releasing the key, she wipes her face to temporarily erase her feelings of hopelessness. She knows that James' actions—if they continue—will most likely cost him his family, but that eventuality will have to wait.

Looking at the clock on the microwave, she sees that it's 5:45. It's time to get the little people ready to begin their day. There is much to do.

She is parked in a place that once held fond memories of wild, carefree times, but she knows she will never return to this parking spot once she makes the decision to leave the truest love she's ever felt. She will be devastated—without question—but more importantly, the two little people that their love created will have two places to live. Her heart sinks at the thought.

Naomi sits back in the heated leather seat and checks the temperature on the dashboard. It's fifty-five degrees. Somewhat chilly for a summer morning. Her eyes move to the time: 6:45 a.m.

Perfect timing, she thinks.

Grabbing her purse, lunch case, and briefcase from the passenger seat, she prepares to exit her vehicle. There are only a few cars parked inside the parking garage, one of them being Norman's black Lincoln MKZ.

Closing her door, she quickly scans his vehicle for any scratches or signs of violence. Seeing nothing, she walks toward the door that will take her inside the building and past the security booth. She walks at a quickened pace in black leather flats. She made sure she wore comfortable shoes just in case she had to move quickly for any reason.

Her head swivels in all directions as she nears the door, watching for anyone else arriving to work. Reaching the door, she takes a deep breath. Today will be a day that she will never forget. Exhaling, she pulls the door open with a smile and enters the building.

Andre and Scott Ferguson are working in the security booth. Things have been even more awkward since Andre confronted her about her fifth-floor activity. She sucks in a large amount of air. What if he has informed the detectives?

No. She knows he would never betray her like that, even though he made it clear he was keeping a sharp eye on her every move.

She quickly and confidently breezes past the booth. "Good morning!" she says in the most cheery voice she can muster.

Neither man speaks, but Naomi can almost feel the daggers, sharp as carving knives, coming from the man who now invades her dreams almost nightly, in wild sex fantasies that she will never share with another soul. Shaking the dream encounters from her thoughts, she turns her gaze from the men who pretend not to notice her. Good. Pretend as though I'm invisible. I will be able to move quicker knowing no eyes are following me. No eyes meet hers.

She continues walking across the mix of tans and creams in the porcelain tile to the trail of royal blue carpeting that leads to the elevators. She exhales as she presses the up arrow, eager to reach the safe haven of her office, away from any distractions or prying eyes.

Since the breaking news story on Saturday morning, she's been on pins and needles, and she's glad that she has beaten the rush of her coworkers into the office. She just can't take the whispers about whether or not the body in the park is Michelle's. She wonders that same thing but is still too afraid to face the fact that it may actually be Michelle. Naomi swallows the lump in her throat.

The elevator doors open, and once inside, she closes her eyes and embraces the silence around her. The familiar "ding" of the elevator tells her it's time for the difficult walk to her office. She opens her eyes and tries to affect an "I'm OK" smile, just in case there's anyone to greet on her floor. Naomi does her best to avert her eyes from the yellow tape across Michelle's office door, and she's glad that no one else is in the hall to witness her last few strides toward her office. With tears brimming in her eyes, Naomi feels the metal of her office doorknob. She quickly pushes the door open so that she can enter her personal haven, where she allows the tears to flow. She leans her back against her office door.

I can't believe I may never see Michelle again. Could I have saved her if I had only answered the phone? She squeezes her eyes tightly closed, willing the tears to stop. She opens her eyes to rays from the morning sun filtering through the blinds in her office. Attempting normalcy, she turns on the overhead light, places her bag and briefcase in the extra chair in the corner of the room, and gets behind her desk to boot up her laptop.

She needs to memorize her alibi workload, just in case any questions come up about her whereabouts after today's adventure. Naomi watches as the screen lights up and her homepage populates.

She gets up from her desk and walks toward her belongings. She pulls out her phone to view Norman's schedule. She doesn't want to be encumbered by carrying her purse, so she grabs her ID, some cash, and a debit card and fills her pockets. Her mace she tucks easily into the front of her bra.

She opens the closet door in her office to reveal a full-length mirror and looks herself up and down. She checks her watch, then turns to face her desk and laptop. The waiting is making her impatient.

Walking away from her reflection, she goes back to her desk and sinks into the smooth, leather chair, enjoying both the comfort and the smell.

"I love this chair," she says aloud. After sitting idle for a few meditative moments, Naomi leans forward and enters her password. Then she opens her daily calendar.

The first thing on her list is to talk to all of her clients and make sure all of her accounts are intact. She begins to pull reports. Next, she will make a few calls and then let her voicemail with a promise to return calls be her response for anyone looking for her today.

If anything serious happens, the important people have my cell phone number, she reassures herself.

She exhales and begins doing the things that need to be done. There are still a few more people the police need to interview, and the buzz is still ablaze around the workplace. Her absence should go unnoticed.

She is just hanging up the phone when someone knocks on her door. Unsure whether or not she really wants to answer it, she stays silent. The second knock is harder and more demanding.

"Come in." Relief washes over Naomi. It's just Amanda.

"Well good morning, Naomi. I just wanted to check on you to see how you were taking the news. And there's been lots of rumors and speculation about who the culprit behind this is. There are other people here who care about you."

Naomi smiles. "That is really sweet of you to be concerned about me. I'm trying to stay hopeful. The identity of the woman in Clinton River Park still hasn't been confirmed by the police or even Norman at this point."

"Maybe they did."

"Maybe they did what?"

"Call Norman to identify the body. The rumor is that the police just asked him to come to the station."

Naomi's heart sinks. The air is gone from the room.

Amanda can clearly see the expression on Naomi's face change from hope to sorrow.

"But that's just what's circling the office. I am sure you are right to be hopeful," Amanda says with sympathetic eyes. And with that, Amanda leaves the room without saying another word.

Amid her overwhelming devastation, rage begins to build behind Naomi's eyes. She has to leave the office now and follow Norman. Instead of tracking him during his normal daily activities, as she first intended, Naomi has to think on her feet and hope that she's prepared for whatever happens next. Grabbing her light jacket, she feels for the car keys in her pocket. She takes a second look at the purse she wanted to leave behind and grabs it too, realizing that now that her plans have changed, she might need something that's in there. Trying to maintain a casual tone, she passes Amanda's open office door.

"Going to lunch and then I have some errands to run. Thanks again for caring, Amanda," she says briskly.

"You're welcome," she hears once she's in front of the elevator.

Naomi takes a quick peek around the hall and veers left and into the stairwell. Jogging down the two flights of stairs, she reaches the door to the main floor. Smoothing herself down, as if to put every hair in place, she pulls the door open and approaches the security booth, breezing by with an easy wave. The guards never even look up.

The wedge between Andre and Naomi was proving to be beneficial. She definitely doesn't need for him to be anywhere near her personal space. Biting her bottom lip, she reminisces about something that only happens in her dreams.

So far, none of the security personnel have been Andre. He must be on cart patrol.

She pushes the door open and enters the stairwell to the parking garage. Making it to the next and final door leading to her car, she pushes that door open as well. Standing in a primarily full parking garage, Naomi is surprised to see that so many of her coworkers decided to park inside today. A full parking lot is good news to her; no one will even notice her missing black Audi. She rushes to her car, scanning the parking spaces to see if Norman's car is still there.

The parking space where his car sat earlier is empty. Frantic to catch up with him, Naomi jumps inside her car and hopes she somehow catches up to Norman.

At that moment, the security patrol cart passes by, scanning the parking lot. There is only one person driving the cart today: Andre. Naomi slides lower in her seat, even though her car windows are darkly tinted.

Once the coast seems clear, Naomi pulls out of her parking space in the opposite direction of the patrol cart. She must avoid Andre by any means necessary. Pulling out of the garage, she heads toward the police station, hoping that Amanda is right and that she'll spot Norman's car. Just the thought has Naomi's stomach in knots. She presses harder on the gas, making sure she doesn't go over the speed limit.

About fifteen blocks from her office, she approaches the police station. Among the parking spaces to the left of the building, she spots Norman's Lincoln.

Shit, she thinks as she cruises past the police station.

She needs to find a decent parking space that will give her the advantage of seeing but not being seen. Her eyes search right and left along both sides of the street. There are a few cars on each side of the street but lots of empty spaces, leaving most vehicles in clear view of the police station.

Naomi spots another black Audi without tinted windows and decides to park directly behind it. Now, there's nothing left to do but wait until Norman exits the building. And forty-five minutes later, Norman's full-bodied frame exits the glass doors of the Detroit police station.

She watches him walk straight to his car without looking around. As soon as he starts his car, Naomi starts hers. She watches as he pulls out of his parking space and turns left. She pulls out of her parking space and makes the same left.

He makes another left a few blocks down, then a right, only to make another left. Naomi follows. Unsure of the destination, her intrigue begins to grow as she realizes they are driving away from the office, not toward it.

Norman takes a service road to a highway, and Naomi follows, allowing two cars between them. He rides the stretch of the highway for just two miles before exiting and turning down a busy street with cars lining both sides. The car directly behind Norman turns at the next intersection, leaving just one car between them as they make their way past a strip of bars and restaurants. Norman pulls up to Coogan's Bar and parks in the first available spot. Naomi notices the Spanish words on some of the signs in the window. A Hispanic bar? Seems out of character for Norman.

Following suit, she parks a few cars away from Norman's. Taking a deep breath, she pulls down her visor and checks her appearance. This will never do, she thinks.

From what she can tell, there is only one entrance in and out of Coogan's. She will immediately be recognized if she walks inside the bar and Norman is anywhere near the door. She can't take the chance.

Opening up her armrest, she pulls out a pair of oversized Valentino sunglasses and places them on her face. Inside her glove box is a head wrap she keeps in her car for bad hair days.

She conceals as much of her hair as possible with the wrap and smiles at her reflection. The sunglasses cover most of her face, and now most of her hair is hidden as well. Just a few long spirals jut from the top and bottom of the wrap.

Relieved that she grabbed her purse at the last minute, she fishes for her seduction red lipstick. It's a color she wears only on special occasions for James when they role play. She relishes in the brief moment of bliss as her mind travels to all the other times when she has worn this red lipstick. After applying the lipstick, she looks at her new appearance in the visor mirror. She doesn't even recognize herself.

It's amazing what a few miscellaneous items and some makeup can do, she thinks.

She looks down at the rest of her wardrobe: black slacks with a lightweight tunic sweater that reaches her upper thighs and a black blazer. She wiggles her toes in her comfortable Sesto Meucci flats.

She knows her wardrobe looks a little businesslike for a local bar, but since Norman walked in wearing a three-piece suit only moments before, she doubts that anyone will think twice about her outfit. It is mid-afternoon. Bars are certainly accustomed to business people grabbing a quick drink after lunch before heading back to work.

Reassuring herself as much as she can, she grabs her purse and opens her door.

The sidewalk along the strip is lively with corporate America mixed in with the people who live downtown and those visiting from neighboring suburbs. People of all shades and classes are roaming the streets. She steps onto the sidewalk and walks behind a few people in casual clothes, laughing and joking about something that she couldn't care less about. She turns toward the bar, and as she opens the door, the light from the sun illuminates her entrance. Several people are sitting at the bar, and some are clustered around small tables. She is glad to see so many people.

A young black woman in a cute little black skirt and V-neck t-shirt approaches her.

"Welcome to Coogan's. You can sit anywhere you'd like. Can I get you anything in particular, suga?"

Surveying the room, she spots Norman at the bar with his back toward her and the door.

"Why sure. I will take a rum and Coke," she says with the best phony, Southern accent she can muster.

The young woman smiles and goes to the bar to get the drink.

Locating a table and chairs only a few feet away from Norman, Naomi sits down. Now that she has a chance to look around, she notices the atmosphere of the bar. This bar, like the street, has a mixed bunch of people. There are a few tables of people, both black and Hispanic, looking as though they had come from an office. There are two white guys and four black males seated at the bar. One of them is Norman.

The young woman in the short skirt sashays her way over to Naomi. "Here's your drink, hon. My name's Camila, if you need anything else."

"Thank you." Naomi drawls convincingly.

Just as Camila walks away, she hears Norman's voice.

"Another scotch on the rocks, Lu," his voice bellows.

A Hispanic man with a mustache and wearing a black V-neck t-shirt is behind the bar. His accent is thick.

"This is your fourth one in like ten minutes, man. What's going on with you? Talk to your friend, amigo."

"I'm in some deep shit, Lu. Too much to share. I don't know if I'm going to make it out of this one."

Lu lifts the bottle of scotch and pours it into Norman's glass.

He immediately takes a healthy gulp, leaving only a small amount in the bottom of the glass, and places it back down on the bar.

"I've just identified my wife's body at the police station morgue. And the police tell me I'm the prime suspect in the case and not to leave town under any circumstances."

Lu stands there silently and dutifully pours another shot into the glass.

Gone at the age of thirty-five, Naomi thinks. Her throat closes, and her grip on her glass of rum and Coke tightens so much she fears she might shatter it.

"Somehow it got out about me teaching her a lesson a time or two. You know how women can be. Sometimes you just have to put them in their place. You know, show them who is boss."

Lu doesn't speak. He just waits patiently for Norman to take another gulp.

Looking up at Lu for certainty, he lifts his glass and takes another large gulp. Norman places the glass down in front of him, tapping the side of the glass to signal Lu for another.

Lu pours.

"Man, that's rough. What are you going to do now?"

"Well, clearly fleeing the country is out of the question." Norman lets out a chuckle.

The liquor is finally beginning to set in, after what must be seven shots, by Naomi's estimate. Naomi ordered her drink for show, but as she looks down at it, she's tempted to indulge herself. Her heart aching, she lifts the glass to her lips and drinks. Not a large gulp, but just enough to fill her mouth. She swallows. The heat of the rum slowly moves down her body as she listens. She tries to keep calm, while inside her heart crumbles in agony for the second friend she couldn't save.

"Aren't you going to ask me if I did it, Lu?" Norman's tone is low and deep with regret.

"A man only says what he wants people to know. It's not my place to ask such questions. I am just a listening ear, amigo."

Norman sits back in his barstool, appearing to think about Lu's words.

At that moment, Naomi realizes that Norman's phone must be buzzing against his hip, because he grabs it and looks down at it. Placing the phone back on his hip, he seems to be ignoring the call. Watching Norman's every movement, Naomi continues to take sips of her own liquid satisfaction. With each swallow, she feels the ache in her chest ease ever so slightly.

Norman is a murderer as far as she is concerned. He neither confirmed nor denied to Lu what the police accused him of doing. Caught in her own thoughts, she faintly hears the buzzing of Norman's phone again.

Norman drinks the last of the contents in his glass before grabbing the phone from his hip and answering. Straining to hear him, Naomi listens intently.

"I thought I told you to never call me on this phone." He is speaking with authority. "I can't meet you right now. Things are beginning to go south."

There is a pause on Norman's side of the conversation. Naomi casually sips her drink, feigning disinterest in her surroundings.

"What do you mean don't worry? My life is in jeopardy. I said, no. Meeting right now isn't a good idea."

Lu has stepped away by now to give Norman a semblance of privacy.

"But . . . wait . . . *what?*"

Stumbling from the barstool, he stands, and with a nod of his head toward Lu he lays cash on the bar and hurries toward the door.

"I'm going to my car now. I'll meet you in the usual spot."

And with that, the door to Coogan's opens and closes. He's gone.

Tossing back the last of her drink, Naomi pulls a twenty from her purse and stands. She has no idea where Norman is going, but she needs to stay close behind. She walks swiftly to the door and opens it, but a glimpse of daylight is all she sees before being struck in the face. Her legs turn to water as she falls back into the open doorway and onto the floor. The next thing she sees is Camila kneeling over her, yelling for someone to call 911.

CHAPTER 11

Standing in a thick fog, she looks around but can't see anything or anyone close.

"Hello?" she calls out. "Can anyone hear me?"

Only silence meets her ears.

"Hello? Can anyone hear me?"

She walks blindly, unable to see what is in front of her. She walks farther. Still seeing nothing through the thick fog. Looking in every direction, she begins to panic and starts running. She just wants to reach something—anything—recognizable. Out of breath, she stops. Stooping over, with her hands on her knees, she sucks in huge amounts of air. She can see something small on the ground. She leans in closer. Is that grass?

Inexplicably, her surroundings start coming into focus. Naomi finds herself looking down at a trail, and as she stands up, the grass and surrounding forest become clearly visible. How has she gotten to a forest? The last thing she remembers is trying to follow Norman out of the bar. Cautiously, she walks forward, taking in all the scenery around her. She can smell the scents of grass and wood in the air.

"Make him pay," comes a whisper.

"Hello? Is someone out there?"

"Make him pay." The voice grows slightly louder.

"Do you need help?" Naomi's feet begin to move just a little bit faster. She knows that voice, if only she could hear it a bit louder. She presses on.

She approaches a large bush and has the distinct impression that someone else is present, but she can't see anyone.

"Make him pay." The voice is crisp and extremely clear. And the voice is angry. Naomi can feel it. She shivers.

Feeling a cold hand grasp her ankle, Naomi screams and looks down to see a brown female hand covered in dirt wearing a familiar gold bracelet. In a panic, Naomi kicks herself free and starts running at full speed through the forest that never changes. As she runs, Naomi spots a white light and heads directly toward it, just as she emerges from her dream state.

***

"Ma'am, can you hear me?"

"Check her pulse."

"Ma'am? Do you know your name?"

Naomi forces her eyes to open. She can feel something cold on her head.

She tries to take in her environment. A bright light is being shone in her eyes. She adjusts her head and sees a gloved hand holding a tiny flashlight. She tries to sit up a little but falls back down.

"Ma'am, do you know where you are?" The man is wearing a uniform. A paramedic.

Naomi sits up slowly, feeling the pain in her head increase as she becomes more upright.

"Can you tell me what happened? Are you able to speak?"

The most Naomi can muster is a groan before Camila's worried face appears. Sincere concern is in her eyes.

"Are you OK, honey?"

Naomi's eyes shift and her head turns away from the eyes penetrating her. She parts her lips to speak but can't remember the fake name she typically gives to men who approach her during after-work outings with her friends. Her lips close. Naomi clears her throat, giving the impression that she wants to speak, then grabs her head in confusion.

Seeing her appear more alert, the paramedic tries again.

"Ma'am, can you tell us your name?"

Naomi's eyes shift. Shit, she thinks.

"My name is Naomi." She speaks clear and crisp without her quickly crafted Southern accent.

"Good, ma'am. My name is Jonathan. Looks like you were struck in the head. Can you tell us anything that happened up until this point?"

Naomi stares blankly at the paramedic. His chocolate skin is young and smooth, and the sincerity in his eyes tells her that he is passionate about his work.

"You may have a concussion, Naomi." Her name rolls smoothly off his lips, making her look down at the bar floor. "Can you tell me anything that happened?"

Naomi opens her mouth to speak, then chooses her words carefully.

"I came in for a drink. Once my drink was finished, I grabbed my purse and headed for the door. Before I could make it completely outside, someone struck me hard enough to knock me back inside the door."

"OK. The police will be here shortly. You will have to repeat your story. I just wanted to test your memory. Then we can take you to the closest hospital to get you checked over." He smiles, nodding his head in the direction of the other paramedic, who hasn't introduced himself.

But she wants nothing to do with the police or a trip to any hospital. And she needs to get out of here fast. She doesn't even want the bartender overhearing her real name since he has probably heard her name before during one of Norman's drunken rants about his wife's best friend. She grabs Jonathan's shoulder, signaling that she is ready to get off of the bar floor. Getting the hint, he allows her to brace herself against him to stand.

"I feel fine." Her legs wobble.

"I don't think you do," Camila and Jonathan blurt out in almost perfect unison.

"And what happened to your accent?" Camila asks.

Naomi ignores her question.

"Accent?" Jonathan's expression is a mixture of concern and curiosity.

"Yes, when she came into the bar, she had a thick Southern accent. But now, there is no sign of it."

Naomi wants so badly to run for the door and avoid any more questions. Concentrating on the door, she speaks again in her normal voice.

"It's honestly just a bump on the head. I would prefer that the police weren't involved, and I'm sure I don't need to go to the hospital. And as for my accent, I lived in the South for most of my childhood, so my accent comes and goes," she lies.

She looks into Camila's eyes and lifts her hands to touch her face, working her way toward the huge knot starting to grow on her forehead. Her eyes search the floor for the sunglasses she remembers wearing. She locates the oversized black sunglasses, snapped in two. Naomi can tell that Camila's eyes have more questions just under the surface. Before another word can be spoken, Naomi starts shuffling toward the door.

"Wait, Naomi. While you are free to go, you still have the blood pressure unit on your arm."

She looks down, seeing the Velcro strap still attached to her arm and removes it without looking back.

"Thank you," are the last words she speaks as the blood pressure unit falls to the floor.

"Wait!" Camila says, just as Naomi pushes open the door. Not acknowledging the young woman's plea, Naomi steps into the daylight.

The hot sun beats down on her, and she suppresses a wave of dizziness. She uses her hands to shield her eyes so that she can locate her car. The street isn't as busy as it was earlier. She wonders about the time. Walking in the direction her eyes lead her, she sees her Audi.

She fumbles for the keyless remote from her purse and unlocks her door, slipping into the driver's seat just as she hears police sirens. She glances at the bar door for anyone coming outside, and in a moment, three police cars pull up in front of the bar. Then she sees Jonathan, the paramedic, exit the bar.

Stepping out of one of the police cars are none other than Officer Stacey Ramsey and Detective Thomas Ryley.

Naomi sits back in her seat, unsure what to do next. She can't hear what Jonathan is saying. She can only assume he's repeating what she told him minutes ago.

Nodding their heads with some sort of understanding, the officers get back in their cars.

Naomi feels a rush of relief as she watches the police cars drive away and Jonathan go back inside the bar. In such a large city, it seems strange to her that the detectives on Michelle's case would show up here. Maybe the cops are on to Norman. Then she remembers that she gave Jonathan her real name. Panic sets in, and then a blinding headache from her head injury starts to overwhelm her. Naomi opens the compartment between the seats, takes out a bottle of Aleve, and swallows two pills dry.

The police will probably head to her office to confirm whether or not she and the Naomi from the bar are one and the same. In her increasing state of paranoia, she fears the police will confront her with a barrage of questions. And right now she has no clue how to answer them.

Naomi starts her car and tries to mentally map out a short cut. She has to get back to her office before the police do. Speeding through mild traffic, Naomi reaches the office building and sees no signs of the police cars. The same parking space she left behind hours ago is still empty, so she pulls in. Her head is pounding, but her adrenaline is giving her the stamina she needs to rush to her office. Legs still wobbly, she surveys the parking garage for Norman's car. She doesn't see it.

She pulls open the stairwell door and swiftly passes through security, not giving any attention to who is behind the counter.

She locates the stairwell and continues her journey up to the second floor. Out of breath and dizzy, she grabs the door handle, closes her eyes to regroup, and takes in a deep breath and smiles, trying to seem casual. There are a few people in the hall walking from one office to the next. No one pays any attention to her or gives her a second look.

With her purse on her shoulder she reaches her office door and inserts her key. Stunned, she realizes her door is unlocked. Her heart begins to pound. When she opens the door, she sees the silhouette of someone sitting behind her desk. She stands inside the door, closing it behind her. Is it Norman?

"Where have you been?"

The voice is familiar but not Norman's.

She flips on the light and sees that it's Andre. There's fire in his eyes.

"I had a long lunch. Why are you sitting in my office with the lights off?" She stands in front of her desk with her arms folded, waiting for Andre to rise.

His eyes penetrate her, and he scans every inch of her body before speaking again.

"And what happened to your head? You look like you've been in an accident. Are you sure you don't want to tell me what's going on?" His voice has softened.

"Please get out of my office!" Naomi's voice jumps three octaves, surprising even herself.

Shock covering his face, Andre stands up, walks around Naomi's desk, and pauses for a moment, looking beyond her eyes and into her soul. He grabs her arm tenderly, and then releases it.

Walking to the door, he grabs the handle and speaks. "This isn't over."

Naomi turns and looks at the door, just as he closes it behind him.

"Shit." She drops her purse into the extra chair in front of her desk.

She opens the closet in her office to show the full-length mirror. For the first time since getting whacked in the head, she surveys herself. Andre is right; she looks a wreck. Still wearing the headscarf she added to her disguise, she removes it, setting her curly hair free.

The bump on her head is huge and quickly changing color. Her red lipstick is smeared across her face. What had she been hit with? And why didn't anyone notice her appearance when she returned to the office?

She takes the makeup bag from her purse and does her best to conceal the bruising and touch up her lipstick. She has watched Michelle perform this same ritual a thousand times to cover up bruises given to her by Norman. Her heart sinks and she stops. She is never going to see Michelle again. Norman confirmed that.

Her hands begin to shake as tears begin to pour, leaving trails through her newly applied makeup. Naomi takes a deep breath to get calm. Now is not the time for her to break down. That will come soon enough. If the police show up today, there can be no evidence of anything out of the ordinary. Wiping the traces of tears from her face, she applies foundation again.

After applications of eye shadow, mascara, and rose petal lipstick, Naomi is satisfied with her appearance once more. Giving her reflection her bravest smile, she closes the closet door and sits behind her desk, waiting for a detective or officer to summon her.

She flips open her laptop and stares at the screen. Of course there is work to be done, but the pain in her head reminds her that she may have a concussion. Opening her desk drawer, out of sheer desperation, she pulls out a bottle of water and takes a Tylenol on top of the two Aleve she took earlier. Looking back at her laptop, she signs into it, going through the motions of her usual routine.

In that moment, she's appreciative of Andre's unexpected intrusion. They haven't spoken since the day he caught her in the stairwell, and she can barely look at him now that he's invading her dreams on a regular basis. She thought cutting off their communication would at least ease her subconscious, but like a lot of things, she was wrong.

Dreams, she thinks, as she remembers her dream of the forest.

"Make him pay," echoes inside her head.

"Oh, he definitely will," she promises to her memory of Michelle.

The knock on her office door comes hours later instead of minutes later like Naomi predicted. She is relieved that she had time to relax before her impending meeting with the detective.

To her surprise, after the knock, no one enters the room. Naomi gets up from her desk and goes to the door. She opens it to find a note with her name on it in cursive at her feet. Mesmerized by her own name and curious about the note, she bends down to grab it.

Never taking her eyes off the slip of paper in her hand, Naomi closes her office door and retreats back behind her desk. Realizing that most of the office has cleared for the day, Naomi looks at the time on her watch: 5:10 p.m.

She flips open the folded slip of paper to read the contents.

We need to talk. Please meet me tonight. A.

Sitting back in her seat, there is no doubt in her mind that "A" is Andre.

She reluctantly gets up from her desk and retrieves her phone from her purse. Going to her contact list, she presses a name and listens to the phone ring.

"Imani, darling, I need a few extra hours tonight. There are leftovers in the fridge for the kids. I will be home pretty late. Please call me if there's anything you need." She ends the message by hanging up the call.

Dropping the phone back into her purse, Naomi begins to collect her things and head out to the only place where she has ever met with Andre outside of work alone. He had bargained her into lunch on a few occasions, but now their friendship seems like a far-off memory, considering the distance between them. There is only one bar and grill where Andre ever wants to have lunch. She's sure that Andre wants to make peace, and of course, she'll accept his apologies. After today's events, she desperately needs a partner to complete her investigation, she admits, rubbing the concealed bump on her head.

With her heart still breaking over the loss of her dear friend, Naomi takes the elevator to the main floor. She waves goodbye to the inattentive security guard who doesn't even lift his head. She desperately hopes that her conversation with Andre will return things to normal with the security team. All the guards seem to be ignoring her at this point. She looks straight ahead and enters the stairwell leading to the parking garage.

Her car is the only one in sight, and she walks quickly in the silence. Reaching her car and getting inside, she thinks about the last time she visited a bar with a smiling, happier Andre. Hopefully, tonight they will clear the air. She will open up to him about her investigation and ask for his help. Justice is bigger than any feelings of lust she may have fabricated in her mind. Michelle is dead and Norman, no matter how wealthy, needs to feel the wrath of taking such a precious life from her.

She drives through the streets of Detroit, empowered by thoughts of the impending justice she is about to bring down with the help of one of the very few people she trusts in her life. With the bar and grill in her sights, she hears the vibration of her phone from the bottom of her purse. She parks in just enough time to grab the phone and see that it's James.

"Well hello there, my love. How was your day today?" she smiles into the phone.

She listens closely as he speaks, noting that he expects to return home Thursday or Friday. Good, she thinks. I need a few days to get concrete information on Norman with Andre's help. He asks if she's heading home, and she's pulled from her thoughts. Her smile fades as she lies again to her husband.

"After the day I've had, I'm just grabbing a quick drink before heading home. Imani has the kids; dinner is already prepared; all is well."

After exchanging "I love yous," they end the call. Though her heart aches when she thinks of his obvious infidelity, her heart aches even more for the loss of the woman who was like a sister to her. She no longer has anyone to share her thoughts and secrets with. Someone has to pay for that mistake.

Dropping her phone into her purse once again, she sits inside her car and turns on the radio. Music always makes her feel better, especially if the right song comes on. Naomi begins to flip through her saved stations. She stops when she hears a familiar voice. It's Anita Baker, singing one of Naomi's old favorites, "Sweet Love."

The song ends and Smooth Doctor Love, in his deep, velvety voice, announces that he has a breaking news story. A car was pulled from the Clinton River with a woman's purse inside. Authorities do not know if this has anything to do with the woman's body found on the trail, who has now been identified as Michelle Greeley, the wife of Norman Greeley, who has been reported to be the main suspect in the pending case. The police are hoping to find a breakthrough in the case based on this new evidence.

Naomi's heart stops as she sinks lower into her seat. Justice for Michelle becomes her entire focus. Nothing can get in her way. She grabs her bag and exits the car to go inside.

The hostess greets her warmly.

"Good evening. Would you like a table for dinner or a seat at the bar?"

"The bar would be fine. Thank you."

She scans the room quickly. No sign of Andre just yet. Might as well order a drink, she thinks.

"What can I get you?" inquires the bartender.

"A glass of chardonnay, please," she smiles at the handsome server.

Her first glass goes down quickly. She is lost in thoughts of her own misery and sadness when she realizes her glass is already empty. She requests another and makes a conscious effort to take her time. She empties her second drink, and there is still no sign of Andre. She looks down at her watch; it's getting close to eight. The sun is finally retreating, and darkness will soon follow. She'll have to go soon. She asks the bartender for another drink, and then pulls out her phone. No missed calls.

She looks around the room again. The crowd is beginning to change, as those in casual shirts and jeans are replacing people in business suits and dresses. The conversations are becoming louder and livelier. Where are you, Andre? After this last glass of wine is finished, I am leaving, she decides.

She's beginning to feel the effects of wine on an empty stomach. She slowly drinks her last glass, trying to keep her senses sharp. When she finally pays her tab it's nine thirty. She heads to the parking lot, confused that Andre didn't show up.

In the darkness, she sees a figure leaning against the driver's side of her car. Her heart is in her throat when she hears the familiar voice.

"Well hello, beautiful. I've been waiting for you."

Feeling the effects of the chardonnay, Naomi smiles and leans against the car as well.

"I've been inside the bar for a couple of hours; you couldn't have been waiting for me," she speaks flirtatiously and rubs her hand down his arm.

Seeing the gloss in her eyes, he smiles. "How many drinks have you had, pretty lady?"

"Only three."

"Too many to drive. Can we talk inside?"

"Inside? I'm not going back inside that bar, Andre. I have two little people waiting for me at home. We'll have to try this again some other time." She presses the unlock button, waiting for him to move.

When he doesn't, she looks him over from head to toe. He's wearing black slacks and a black crewneck shirt. Lord, this man is delicious. Her mind flashes to lustful images from her dreams. He catches her eyes and she looks away quickly.

"I meant inside your car, not the building." His voice is sultry.

"Get in." She speaks low, knowing she needs him on her side.

Once both doors are closed, they sit in silence for a moment, both of their minds seemingly distracted by other matters.

Then she speaks. "Sliding that note under my door, then not showing up tonight . . . what game are you playing now?"

"No games. Just wanted to see you, and I know we haven't been on the best of terms lately. This is the last place we were able to talk. I knew I wouldn't have to tell you where to come."

She blushes, looking out her window.

"Look at me," he demands.

Her eyes immediately meet his. She watches him survey her body. In an instant, he leans in and kisses her. Lost in the moment, a groan escapes her lips. Her eyes are closed and she leans into him, sharing the taste of chardonnay still on her lips. Their kiss lasts far longer than she expects. She feels his hands on her body, and the desire living inside of her burns with urgency.

He unbuttons her slacks and slides his hand over the top of her pink and black striped panties to massage her clit.

She begins to moan; her eyes closed tightly.

His slow strokes gradually increase in pace, and she arches her hips up from the seat, giving in to her own temptation, not wanting him to stop.

Her eyes open to see him staring down at her with a mischievous grin.

Looking deep into her eyes, he slips the crotch of her panties to the side and inserts two fingers inside her now throbbing wetness.

Never unlocking their eyes, she begins to grind against the hand giving her pleasure. Breathing heavy, she allows herself to indulge deeper in this moment. She is about to climax, when he stops and sits back in the passenger seat.

Seeing his manhood so rock-hard through his pants, desire fills her, and her wetness turns into a fountain. Her hand reaches out and grabs him. Now it's his turn to groan in pleasure. She can't take her eyes off his hardness, and she unzips his pants to free it. Licking her lips, she bends down and begins pleasuring him with her mouth, like she has done so many times in her dreams. It feels so good to swallow him whole.

He reclines his seat as her head moves up and down, slowly at first, then her tempo begins to build.

"Shit, Naomi."

She smiles with her lips wrapped around his now throbbing manhood. Satisfied with the built up pressure, she stops and sits back in her seat.

"Take off your pants, please," he begs, his lust catching in his throat.

She smiles and lifts her hips from the seat to remove her bottoms, feeling the warm, relaxing effects of the chardonnay.

She throws her leg across the passenger side and mounts him with ease.

He gasps, grabbing her hips to direct her pace to a slow grind, allowing her to feel every wave he creates. His eyes penetrate her soul, matching her rhythm as she rides, refusing to break eye contact.

Her eyes close once more, and she begins to whisper his name, like she has done in fantasy after fantasy. Feeling herself on the verge of climax once again, she quickens the pace of her ride.

Their moans become a song they both sing until they climax, one after the other.

Out of breath, Naomi returns to her side of the car, feeling a sense of relief after one of the most stressful days of her life.

Andre fixes his pants.

Neither of them speaks for what seems like a lifetime.

Lost in her thoughts, Naomi stares out her window, not wanting to look at him. She wants him to speak first. She knows he has questions for her. Instead, what she hears is his car door opening. Her eyes turn toward him. He's staring at her with intense fire in his eyes, and then he exits her car. She leans her head against the glass window, which feels wonderfully cool under her burning skin, and slides her pants back on. Looking around at the cars still in the parking lot, she is grateful for the dark tint of her windows.

After a few more minutes, she starts her car. For the moment, she is blissful, leaving all of her cares, worries, and broken heart in the back of her mind. Not sure what to make of the weakness she has told herself repeatedly not to give into, she decides to worry about the consequences of tonight's pleasure later. For now, she will bask in the feeling of euphoria that sex often gives her. She looks at her clock: 10:30 p.m. Shit. It's time to get home to the people who love her unconditionally.

The pleasure she has experienced is more than she expected but what scares her the most, as she feels the tingle between her thighs, is that she wants it again.

Speeding off into the night, she allows her thoughts to drift toward flashbacks of the passion that has her biting her bottom lip in amusement. Now, she has most certainly gained an ally, though this isn't the way she planned to secure his loyalty. Not completely sober, she can't help but smile. Her rekindled friendship with Andre has turned into something a bit more. And she likes it.

CHAPTER 12

Naomi enters her house through the inside garage door and tiptoes lightly through the kitchen, looking in adoration at the scene before her. The kitchen has been cleaned beyond perfection, and as she walks into the living room, she sees Imani sleeping peacefully on the sofa. It would be a shame to wake her, Naomi thinks, grabbing the blanket from the end of the sectional. She covers the young woman, who only slightly stirs when the blanket touches her.

Naomi returns to the kitchen and pulls her wallet from her purse, taking out a hundred-dollar bill like she does every time Imani stays late. She looks at the clock on her stove. It's after eleven. She walks back into the living room and places the bill on the coffee table so that Imani will see it in the morning.

Satisfied, she goes upstairs to peep in on the little people. At the top of the stairs, she's greeted by two distinctive light snores, and she can't help but smile as she reaches the half opened bedroom door. As she looks in, both children are fast asleep in their own beds, stretched out completely in different directions. Her heart swells. She loves them so much it aches. She enters the room to look closer at her tiny blessings, kissing each one.

"Happy dreams, my loves," she whispers in the darkness before heading out of their room. With a sense of overwhelming gratitude, she continues down the hallway to her master bedroom. Pushing the door open, she removes her top and then her pants. Realizing that she has no underwear on, she reaches into her pants pocket where she stuffed them before getting out of the car. Grabbing her clothes, she throws them into the dirty clothes hamper on her way to the bathroom.

She turns on the shower. As the bathroom begins to fog, she inspects every inch, every curve of her body in the bathroom mirror. She is beautiful, clothed and unclothed. She doesn't step inside the shower until she can no longer see her reflection clearly.

Stepping into the steaming water, she sighs with a sense of desperately needed relaxation. She washes the makeup from her face, closing her eyes as she puts her entire head under the stream of water. She reaches up to feel the bump on her head. It is still sore but, to her relief, it seems to be going down. With a little luck, any bruising will be minimal and easy to cover with makeup. With her eyes closed under the water and her fingers in her hair, flashes of her indiscretion with Andre come without warning.

She rubs her hands down her body until she reaches the pearl between her legs. Slowly stroking herself, she thinks about the way he touched her, the way her body shivered in response to foreign hands on it. After her climax, she grabs her washcloth and bathes, her mind a collection of thoughts that amount to nothing.

After she is clean, she steps out of her shower, grabs her bath towel, and exits the bathroom into her master bedroom. She wraps the towel around her soaking wet hair and sits on the side of the bed. One tear falls, then two, and then three, until Naomi is sobbing. She cries for many reasons. She cries for her marriage; she cries for Michelle; she cries for her children; she cries for the deep hatred in her heart; she cries for her moment of weakness.

Finally able to let out all of her emotions, she cries feverishly for all of her current troubles until her eyes seem as though they might close from swollenness. Curling up in her bed alone, naked, and still damp, her cries continue until sleep eventually takes her from the madness that has become her life.

Her eyes open before sunrise, just like every morning. But this morning is different from all the rest. Her eyes remain slightly puffy from her night of tears. Lying on her side, she rolls onto her back to stare at the beautifully crafted ceiling. She had specifically requested crown molding when they purchased the home, she remembers.

A few more lonely tears escape her eyes. From now on, every day when she wakes up, she has to face the reality that Michelle is dead. Murdered. A few more tears fall. Naomi closes her eyes tightly in an attempt to will them away.

Her world has been turned upside down in a matter of weeks, and after her indulgence with Andre, Naomi knows things aren't going to get any clearer. Her legs quiver as her mind returns to those penetrating eyes, the grip of those strong hands. Feeling her arousal, she opens her eyes and sits up in bed.

No. No more fantasies. One night of sex should have at least satisfied you enough to stop the fantasies, she says to herself. Now, get up and act like you have responsibilities.

Following her own instructions as if she could hear them in her mother's commanding voice, she pulls the covers back. Exchanging the towel she slept in for a sleep shirt, she walks out of her room and down the hall, trying not to wake her children. It is definitely too early to start getting them ready for daycare. Plus, she wants coffee and silence while she gets her day in order.

She walks down the stairs carefully, expertly avoiding the two squeaky stair treads that she's committed to memory, and enters the living room. Through the window she sees a police car parked on the opposite side of the street. Has she been assigned a watchman?

Naomi is both surprised and confused. Why would the police issue a protective detail? Standing there in the window, racking her brain for an explanation, Naomi feels a migraine coming on.

Maybe the police are really going to extreme measures now that Norman is their primary suspect. Is Norman coming for me next? How would he know I am on to him? Maybe Lu recognized my name after all.

Despite their unusually heavy presence, Naomi isn't going to leave her friend's murder in the feeble hands of the police. It is definitely time to get Andre involved. He can help her elude the cops, and—in case things take a turn for the worse—someone needs to know where she is at all times. Andre's the only one she can trust right now. And even though temptation got the better of her last night, it doesn't mean sex has to continue, she lies to herself.

Backing out of the living room, Naomi heads for the kitchen to make coffee without flipping any light switches. Naomi has plenty to stress over, to cry about, to get overwhelmed about, but this morning she needs to stay focused. She stands in front of the coffee maker, concentrating on the drops as they hit the inside of one of her favorite mugs.

Her plan is to have a normal day at work, then after hours, visit the Greeley home to look for foul play of any kind. Her new police detail might make this evening's venture difficult; that's where she hopes Andre can help.

He also seems adamant about talking to her as well, based on the note that he slid under her door. She assumes that it's related to her mysterious behavior since Michelle's disappearance, but she could be wrong. Weighted by curiosity, Naomi grabs the already sweetened coffee and sips.

"Mmm." She closes her eyes.

If this morning's coffee is any sign of how the day is going to pan out, things will go smoothly. After half the cup is emptied, the first rays of the morning sun flicker through the trees outside the kitchen windows. Naomi puts her coffee on the kitchen counter and checks the sofa to see if Imani is still there. Seeing only a ruffled blanket, she retreats upstairs to the spare bedroom and wakes up Imani. It's time to start hustling the kids up for their morning routine.

Standing in her bathroom, Naomi finishes the final touches of her lightly applied makeup for the natural appearance she is going for. Then she hears small steps running down the hall, final destination: her master bathroom. She turns to greet them with a smile as they reach her doorway in unison. They're wearing the clothes Imani picked out for them.

Two pairs of groggy eyes look up at her, with the same question.

"Mommy put oatmeal on the counter for you two. Head downstairs, and I will be right behind you."

Without saying a word, they turn around together to head downstairs.

"Mommy loves you," Naomi adds. She applies the finishing touches to her lipstick and then stares at herself in the mirror. Giving herself a nod of approval, she walks out of the bathroom and slides her feet into her wedges as she crosses her bedroom.

She pauses at her mirror to check her appearance. Her Alice and Olivia dress is gray and flowy—striking just the right chord. The dress's shiny silver buttons make a line down her front that stops just above her navel. Underneath is one of her favorite black bras and on her feet are black suede wedges that fit her feet comfortably. She looks casual and effortless. Satisfied with her appearance, she admires her reflection, and makes her way to the kitchen just as the doorbell rings.

Both of her children's heads spring up at the sound.

She smiles at her babies, and then speaks.

"Finish up your oatmeal so we can get ready to go. Daniel, help your sister into her jacket after you put the bowls in the sink."

She shouts up to Imani, "Come downstairs as soon as you are done, Imani. I left a banana and apple on the counter for you if you want to take a snack with you."

Daniel nods his obedience as he shovels the last of his oatmeal into his mouth.

Naomi heads toward the front door, assuming it's the officer who was parked outside this morning. She waits for a second ring before reaching for the door handle. She opens the door to a young black male, with boyish good looks, in a police uniform.

He smiles at her gaze.

"Good morning, ma'am. My name is Officer Michael Carter. It has been brought to my commanding officer's attention that your best friend was murdered. Until we understand more about the case, I've been assigned to keep you safe. Please carry on with your day like you normally would. I will stay in close range of you at all times," he finishes, waiting for her sign of understanding.

The officer clears his throat, and waits for his instructions to be understood.

Naomi smiles sweetly, and extends her beautifully manicured hand.

Accepting her gesture of sincerity, Officer Carter smiles and takes her hand in his.

"Would you have some coffee brewing? I'm in desperate need of a refill."

"Why sure, Officer Carter. Come on in." She moves out of the doorway to allow him to enter then leads him into the kitchen. She heads straight for a cabinet and pulls out a gray and white striped mug.

"Kids, say good morning to Officer Carter."

Between giggles, Daniel and Serena bid their visitor good morning.

"Good morning," Officer Carter says, appearing to study every detail of the room.

Naomi's recently remodeled kitchen has white marble counters and black cabinetry. Her kitchen looks like it came from a catalog, save for a scratch here and there, courtesy of her two children. With a knowing smile, Naomi turns around with the mug in her hand and speaks.

"The kitchen was recently remodeled. Nice work, right?"

"Nice is an understatement, don't you think?"

Naomi presses the button on her Keurig and waits for his cup of coffee to brew.

"Not sure how you take your coffee, officer, but the creamer is in the fridge and the sweetener is in the pantry." She nods to both places and hands him the mug.

"Thank you, ma'am."

Turning her attention to the island where her two little people sit, she gives instructions.

"Daniel, take your bowls to the sink and get your jackets. It's just about to time to go."

Grabbing the two bowls and scooting off the stool, he passes her to get to the sink. She smiles as her eyes follow his every step. They aren't so bad, my two minions, she thinks. Naomi grabs her purse and briefcase and motions to the officer to follow her out the door.

"You can take the mug with you. I highly doubt you'll steal it," she adds playfully.

In front of her, she watches as Daniel, already wearing his favorite blue jacket, helps Serena into her favorite pink one.

"Grab your bags from the stairs and let's head out, troops."

For the first time, she hears him laugh. She turns around

quickly. "What, the officer has a sense of humor?" She smiles, all her teeth showing.

"You have some adorable kids."

"Well, thank you. Come on you two, we will go through the garage. Officer Carter will go out the front door. I expect you'll be en route, officer?"

Naomi calls again for Imani to come downstairs. Emerging quickly with one arm in her jacket and bag in hand, Imani rushes by them to get to the kitchen. Grabbing the promised fruit from the counter, she bolts for the door without noticing the officer.

"Well good morning, young lady."

Imani turns on her heels and looks at him.

"Good morning, sir." She bats her eyes due to his physique and then smiles at Naomi. "See you tonight, Mrs. T!"

Officer Carter nods as he walks past them to get to the front door. Naomi turns to follow the officer and opens the front door for him.

"Don't forget to lock up," she hears him say before she closes the door and locks it securely.

Daniel and Serena are already in the garage, fussing over who will sit behind mommy in the car. She clears her throat and presses the unlock button on the fob for her midnight blue BMW.

"Get into your seats now, please."

Silence falls over them and they both hop into the car. Waiting and eyeing them closely, she watches as her instructions are followed. Grabbing the back door to close it, she adds, "Put on your seatbelts."

She backs slowly out of the garage, thinking to herself what an eventful day today is going to be. As she drives down the residential streets, she looks in her review mirror. Officer Carter is following not far behind.

***

After dropping the kids off at daycare, Naomi heads for work and parks her car in the outside parking lot of her building, watching as Officer Carter parks a few cars down from hers. She collects her things from the passenger seat and gets out. Closing the door with her hip, she half expects the officer to join her as she enters the building. But there is no sign that he's going to exit his vehicle, so she begins her walk toward the door.

Breezing through security, she doesn't look in one direction or the other. Safely making it to the sanctuary of her office, she lets out a breath of reassured satisfaction. She has barely put down her belongings when she hears a knock at her office door.

CHAPTER 13

Without waiting for Naomi's response, Andre turns the knob and steps inside her office. He closes the door behind him, and Naomi hears the lock turn.

She is standing in front of her desk and has every intention of sending him away—how dare he just open the door and walk in? But his steps are large and swift and before she can open her mouth to say anything, his lips are on hers, paralyzing every muscle in her body instantly. Allowing the kiss to penetrate her, she gives in to the warmth that begins to consume her.

His hands are gripping her with intensity. He has invaded her thoughts for the last twenty-four hours; she can't bring herself to resist. A moan escapes her lips.

Finding his way to the buttons on the front of her dress, he stops kissing her and unbuttons the first two to expose her perfectly rounded breasts. He caresses the V-shape created by her cleavage and she shudders. There is fire in his eyes as he smiles at her excitement. Never losing the smile, he gets on his knees and lifts the hem of her dress, starting from the bottoms of her calves and ever so slowly inching her dress upward. Her legs shake. Before him is an unexpected surprise: Naomi isn't wearing any underwear. Beautiful in its own creation, Andre admires her impeccable smoothness.

Naomi's eyes open to look down at him. His hands have stopped moving. When she looks into his eyes, the fire penetrates the deepest part of her.

He takes her in his mouth in that moment.

She has to grip the edges of her desk to steady herself as she willfully stifles her moans. Her eyes are closed tightly, as she enjoys the wonder that is him.

Just as she is about to climax, he stops, lifting his face to reveal the wetness that he created all over the bottom half of his face. Standing up, he begins unbuckling his belt buckle to display a fully rock-hard eight inches, throbbing ever so lightly, every few seconds.

With hunger in her eyes, Naomi drops to her knees. She swallows him whole. He groans. She sucks him slowly, forcing him to savor every moment, then she starts to speed up. All he can do is groan until he can wait no longer. Pulling her to her feet and pushing her onto the end of her desk, he lifts her legs and enters her warm wetness. He kisses her as he deepens his stroke, muffling the sounds that erupt from her as he sinks deeper inside. The pace he created increases dangerously; it is all Naomi can do to keep from bursting with ecstasy.

A few strokes later, they have reached the point of no return. Instead of spraying the inside of her fortress, Andre steps back and allows his orgasm to explode onto her fifteen-hundred-dollar rug.

Coming down from the euphoric cloud that fills the room, Naomi is finally able to catch her breath.

Still panting, Andre puts his manhood back into its proper place, and in a daze, pulls up his pants.

Naomi leans against her desk to steady herself on legs that have turned to water from the unexpected and inviting orgasm.

Eyeing the empty second chair in her office, Andre sits.

"Well, now that we have that settled. What have you been up to, '*Detective Tanner?*'" Andre questions jokingly.

She smiles at his cop remark. "I don't know how I'm supposed to talk to you after all of this. I need a few hours. Maybe more than a few."

She fights with her wobbly legs as she forces herself to gain control and make it around the desk to sit comfortably.

"You have to leave my office." Her voice is low and her eyes never meet his—could not meet his.

"Naomi, we need to talk."

"And we will, Andre. Just not right now. I am too distracted to have a methodical conversation with you right now."

His smile is devilish when he speaks.

"If I would've known this was all I needed to do to keep you quiet, this would have happened years ago."

"Get out," she blushes.

Obliging her request, Andre calmly stands up and brushes imaginary dust from the front of his pants.

"I guess you're throwing me out then. We are talking later. Meet me at the bar."

"Can we actually do lunch instead? I have something I'm trying to get to tonight, which is mostly the reason we need to talk."

"Lunch it is. Don't keep me waiting, beautiful." And with that, he exits her office.

Naomi puts her head on the desk as her legs quiver in defiance. The taste of him still on her lips, she licks them. How did she forget her underwear this morning? Her mind slowly plays back the pleasurable last few minutes. How long was he in here? she wonders, as she opens her laptop to look at the time: twenty minutes. Twenty minutes felt like so much longer; flashes of his lips illuminate her thoughts.

Focus, dammit, she commands herself. Your mission is too far from completion to slip up. Entering her password, she gains access to her files so she can actually get some work done today. After about an hour of typing, organizing, and calculating, Naomi gets up from her desk for a stretch and picks up her purse and briefcase. She opens her office closet and pauses to look at her reflection in the mirror. Her top two buttons are still unbuttoned. She buttons them. Hanging up her belongings, Naomi grabs her phone and walks back to her chair. Sitting down, she places her phone to the right of her laptop and begins typing her third report.

Grabbing her phone, she scrolls through her contacts until she finds Andre's phone number.

Meet me at the Olive Garden by the movie theater at 11:30, she types and sends to Andre before putting her phone back down.

There is so much to tell Andre that she doesn't even know where to begin. She can start with the sex she overheard or maybe about the few pieces of evidence she has found. Maybe she can start with what happened to her at the bar.

Taking a break in her work, Naomi thinks about what she will say. She can just start talking and whatever comes out is what she will say. She knows she may have to skip a few details for the sake of her own sanity. She can't tell him about the park. She feels crazy for thinking that someone was watching her from the shadows.

And she probably shouldn't share her interview with the detective and the officer. But she has to tell him about Officer Carter. He'll be on her tail as soon as she leaves the office, which is why she arranged to meet Andre rather than ride together. Though taking separate cars isn't at all unusual for the two of them. And although they'd always shared an intense chemistry, nothing more had happened other than a kiss on the cheek. But now . . . she swallows the lump in her throat. Her legs quiver in remembrance.

She dares not think about it. They are meeting in a public place, around a lot of people, with her detail following close behind. There is no chance of seclusion.

Naomi finds comfort in the thought that she has things completely under control, but they won't stay that way if she keeps giving in to the intense fire she feels in her body when his sexy eyes look her over hungrily. Now she knows what's in store. Before they were only fantasies that played tricks with her mind, allowing her imagination to run rampant. She could dismiss fantasies, but the real thing is a lot harder to ignore.

She stares at her laptop screen.

Perhaps she is so wrapped up in her own pain and suffering that she has allowed herself to be vulnerable with someone who was almost as close to her as Michelle. He may be all she has left, as far as true friends, if the truth about James finally rears its ugly head. She has no idea about these women who have been texting him, but clearly he has some affairs in the works. Unintentionally, she has started her own affair. Feelings she has so easily dismissed before are now alarmingly real. She trusts Andre more than she trusts James at the moment.

Wiping the thoughts from her mind, she begins to focus on work. Her assignments aren't going to complete themselves. Thirty minutes into her vigorous work, Naomi gets a knock on her door.

"Meeting in five minutes," Amanda says, popping her head into the door before waiting for a response.

"Coming," Naomi sings in a delightful voice.

Things feel seemingly normal, if only for just a moment at a time. Exactly what she needs, normalcy, she thinks as she heads out of her office, away from the place that she considers to be her safe haven.

After downing their first drinks at the lunch table, Naomi begins to tell Andre everything that has happened up until this point, minus a few details here and there.

"So that's what I was doing when you saw me in the stairwell the other day. And this is from the unfortunate punishment I received the other day," she adds, pulling her hair back to reveal the remains of the bump on her forehead. Then she remembers to pull out her cellphone and show him the photo of Norman's schedule.

"This is the schedule that lead me to the knot on my head. If you look closely, you can see all the details of each day. He only has a few meetings noted, which makes me wonder what he didn't write down and how much time that gives me. Look, Andre, I need your help."

Sitting back in his chair, he grabs his second drink and downs it. He stares at her for a moment before speaking.

"So what's our next move?"

Naomi smiles, then leans into the table slightly.

"I want to go to their estate, to see if Michelle left any clues behind. Norman has some important dinner tonight, so he will definitely be away from the house. I will probably have to have Imani spend the night with the kids. But I'll pay her double, and everyone wins."

Andre doesn't speak.

"I also have a police detail," she announces. "Evidently, the detective assigned someone to watch my back until they know more about what happened to my best friend."

"Police detail? How the hell are you supposed to sneak into someone's house and you have a cop following you around everywhere you go? I take it he is somewhere in the parking lot now? Or maybe he's inside this restaurant lurking behind a corner? You are taking too much of a risk here. Sometimes it's better to just walk away from things."

"I'm not walking away from anything, goddammit." She slaps her fist on the table, rattling the empty glasses. "You are going to help me. We just need to figure out how."

Just then her phone rings. Looking down at the screen, she sees James' name.

Naomi's and Andre's eyes meet.

"Before you answer that," Andre utters in a low tone. "I have been meaning to just come out and voice my feelings for you but the timing never seemed right."

Scooting back from the table, Naomi looks for the nearest exit, hearing what Andre is saying but wanting to get this call over and done with more. By the time she reaches the sidewalk, she has just missed the call. Pressing the name on the screen, she calls him back immediately. As she lifts the phone to her face, she sees Officer Carter's car parked across the street, but no one is inside. Shit, she thinks. Andre may have been right about him lurking around every corner.

James answers on the third ring.

"Hey love," she says first. She hears rustling, and then he speaks into the phone.

"Hey babe. I was just calling to see how your workday was going and say that I love you."

She smiles at the phone before she answers. Then in the background, she faintly hears a woman's voice announce, "I think strawberries might be my favorite fruit." The phone rustles again and Naomi is at a loss for words, her heart stricken with pain.

"Hello?" he asks.

"Who was that?"

"Who was who?"

There is a brief silence.

"Oh Naomi, that was just room service, dropping off the strawberries I ordered to go with my brunch special. The room service in this hotel is past amazing."

In her gut, she knows he's lying. She is too afraid to speak, for fear that her voice will crack. She swallows hard.

"Naomi? You still there?"

"Umm, yeah, but I gotta go."

"Baby, wait, I . . ."

She disconnects the call and turns around to go back inside the restaurant. Before she can open the door, her phone vibrates in her hand. Ignoring it, she enters the restaurant and scans the room for Officer Carter, spotting him at the bar. She rushes past, not wanting to be seen and heads straight for the restrooms.

He looks up as she passes him.

Just as she's about to enter the ladies' restroom, she hears her name.

"Naomi!"

She turns around to face Andre, barely able to hold back the tears of her broken heart. She doesn't speak; she just stares at the warm face in front of her. Andre gently guides her away from the door and caresses her cheek.

"You don't have to tell me what's going on; just let me mend your broken heart." He kisses her lightly at first but then with more intensity. Then he stops. "I want you to know that I'm in; however you need my help in bringing down Norman. I would do almost anything for you." He takes her in his embrace and lets her rest her head on his chest.

"As for James, if he makes you this unhappy you can always end things with him and spend the rest of your life with me," Andre continues. "I would love to meet your kids. I'm sure you are an amazing mother to them."

But his words fall on deaf ears. Naomi is too caught up in her agony. She allows her head to remain on his chest as a few more tears escape, and then finds enough comfort in his arms to briefly get herself together. She lifts her head, and clears her throat to speak.

"Just let me freshen up, and we can go back to work. I'll fill you in on more of my plan away from a place that's so crowded.

Also, I spotted the officer in the restaurant, so we have to be smart about the next steps we take."

Andre appreciates this distraction. "Which one is he?"

Waiting for a woman to pass by on her way to the restroom, Naomi pauses then answers, "He's the one wearing a navy blue striped polo shirt and khaki slacks at the bar."

Appearing to make a mental note of this, Andre releases Naomi from his embrace.

"Head into the restroom, and I'll meet you back at the table. Once you come out, I'll have paid our bill and be ready to head for the door."

Nodding her head, she agrees with him. Her face must be streaked with tears, and it's only lunchtime. She still has half of the day ahead of her before her night excursion with Andre. Forcing her mind back to the task at hand, she steps away from Andre, gives him a quick smile, and then enters the restroom. When she comes back out a few minutes later, another scan of the room reveals that the officer is still sitting at the bar.

He raises a glass that looks like gin and tonic, but Naomi knows better. She nods her head in his direction then walks back to the table where Andre is waiting. As soon as she reaches the table and sits down, Andre speaks.

"So that's him?"

"Yep."

"Ready to go?"

"I most certainly am. I'll call you in the car and fill you in on how I think we can get around Officer Michael Carter tonight. James will probably be spending an extra night out of town, so tonight will be the perfect night."

Andre rises from his seat. "Lead the way, my lady."

After returning to their cars, Naomi watches as Officer Carter heads casually to his police car and gets inside. She pulls out of the parking lot and presses the button on her dashboard to call Andre on speaker so that she can talk and drive.

CHAPTER 14

Pulling into her driveway for the night, Naomi watches as Officer Carter pulls up in front of her house and turns off his lights. Rolling the plan in motion, Naomi grabs her car door and exits. Instead of taking the entrance into her kitchen, Naomi walks down her driveway and heads toward the police car parked on the street. She sees the outline of Officer Carter's head tilt to the right, and she knows he's watching her approach from his rearview mirror. When she finally reaches his door, he lowers his window.

"Would you like to come in to use the restroom, get a drink or water, or even grab a small blanket from inside since you intend on spending the night out here?"

He looks up at her from the driver's seat and smiles.

"The restroom sounds perfect. I was wondering if I was going to have to piss on one of these beautiful trees by your house."

"You are more than welcome to come inside," she offers pleasantly.

The officer follows her back inside the garage and through the kitchen entrance of the home. Naomi presses the button by the door to close the garage.

Walking through the house, she doesn't see Imani on the couch and assumes she has gone to the guest bedroom for the night after putting Naomi's kids to bed. Naomi reminds herself to check on them before she heads out for the night just to make sure everything is in order.

"The bathroom is around the corner and to your left." She walks to the refrigerator and grabs the pitcher of filtered water, then she grabs two glasses from the cabinet.

In a drawer beneath the cabinets, Naomi keeps lorazepam, an anti-anxiety medication prescribed by her doctor to help her whenever she's on the verge of a panic attack. She takes three from the bottle, grabs a knife from the holder on the counter, and crushes the pills quickly.

At that moment, Officer Carter comes into view.

"Would you like a glass of water or coffee to take back to your car?"

"Just a glass of water is fine for now. I wired up on caffeine at the coffee stand outside your office building."

Sliding the crumbled pills into her hand as discreetly as possible, Naomi walks over to the pitcher with her fist closed tightly. Grabbing the pitcher, she walks back over to the glasses and brushes the contents from her fist into a glass, then adds water. Pausing to let the medication dissolve, she turns and hands the glass to Officer Carter.

She pours a second glass for herself and drinks while he holds his glass in his hand.

"This water should filter out some of the coffee I've been pounding for the last hour." He drinks the water in four large gulps and hands the glass back to Naomi.

"Well, I'm glad I could reduce the acid that you have filled your body with on an empty stomach."

Just then, Imani appears in the hallway leading to the kitchen.

"Well hello there, honey."

"Hey Mrs. T, I was just making sure it was you down here. I heard voices and came to check it out."

"Thank you so much for staying the night again tonight, sweetheart. I appreciate you these last few nights."

"Hello Officer Carter. I am going back upstairs; just wanted to make sure that everything is OK."

"Yes, everything is fine. Can you pop your head into the kids' room, just to make sure that they are still out for the night?"

"Yes ma'am," she responds groggily as she heads back upstairs.

Officer Carter's eyes trail in the direction of Naomi's and he smiles.

"Before everyone in this house wakes up, let's get you back to your cruiser, Officer Carter," Naomi suggests, escorting him toward the front door.

Naomi watches as the officer retreats back to his vehicle. She waits until he is inside his car before giving him a friendly wave and closing the front door. The medication should start making him extremely drowsy in about twenty minutes, she estimates.

Turning all the locks on the door, she grabs the blanket from the couch, folds it in silence, and throws it over one of the arms of the couch.

Imani is such a sweet girl, Naomi thinks as she heads upstairs to check her little ones for herself.

Peeking into the partially cracked door, she looks in on her two wild sleepers, sprawled out like starfish on their beds. She closes the door to just a sliver before heading to her master suite to prepare for her home invasion with Andre. Realizing she left her phone downstairs, Naomi quickly heads downstairs to the kitchen. Looking around, she remembers that she left her belongings in her car when she walked over to Officer Carter's cruiser.

Going into the garage, she opens her driver's side door and reaches for her bags. Walking back in with them casually in her hand, she sits them down on the kitchen island. Finding her phone, she swipes through her text messages in search of Andre's name. Selecting his name, she types her message.

Start heading this way. I'll be ready in a minute. And don't forget about the lights, just in case.

After pressing send, she heads back upstairs with her phone gripped tightly in her hand. Back inside her room, she begins to undress. She has about thirty minutes before Andre arrives, and she needs time to mentally prepare herself for what she is about to do.

Out of habit, she drops her clothes at the foot of her bed and enters her bathroom to jump in the shower. The steaming hot water feels so good; she almost doesn't want to get out. The bathroom begins to fog, and she grabs the soap to cleanse her body from today's workday.

Other events begin to flash in her mind; in particular, the spontaneous, passionate sex this morning with Andre. She couldn't have stopped herself from indulging in his advances this morning even if she wanted to, considering the previous night was so hot and fresh on her skin and the endless dreams that invade her sleep.

She rubs soap in random places all over her body, as she allows her mind to drift in the hot water. Her eyes open as she rinses off the soap and turns off the water. As she exits the shower, she grabs her towel from the hook, wraps it around her body, and then steps back into her bedroom. The clock on her nightstand reads 10:45 p.m.

She walks to her dresser and pulls out a black, long-sleeved cotton shirt and black yoga pants, along with black undergarments, and gets dressed. For her feet, she chooses Cole Haan black ballerina flats. After all, a cat burglar can still look classy, she thinks. Standing in front of her full-length mirror, she looks herself over. Giving her reflection a smile of approval, she heads back to the bathroom to coax her curly hair into a bun.

Now it's time to stretch, she thinks. Practicing a few of her yoga poses, she stretches her body to get her muscles warm and limber. Sitting on the floor of her bedroom, she lifts her head to check the time: 10:55 p.m.

She hops to her feet, grabs her cellphone from the bed, and peeks in on Imani and the kids before heading downstairs. She walks in short, quick steps down the stairs and into the kitchen, trying to be as quiet as she can. She walks over to her belongings on the kitchen island and grabs her mini pink flashlight, her mace, some leather gloves that are stashed year-round at the bottom of her purse, and her spare house key that she keeps on a silver key chain.

With the items in her hands, she heads for the front door and turns each lock slowly and quietly. Pulling open the front door, she holds her breath while the alarm system emits its familiar chime signaling that the door has been opened and exhales before stepping out into the night.

Thankful that she never turned the porch light on, she locks the front door with her key and pauses on the porch while her eyes get accustomed to the darkness. She looks for any signs that Officer Carter is somehow still awake. From where she is standing, he doesn't appear to be moving, but for her own reassurance, she needs a closer look.

As she is about to step away from the porch and head toward the police cruiser, her phone vibrates in her hand. Ignoring it, she clips her mace, key, and flashlight onto the purely cosmetic belt loops on her yoga pants. Still holding the gloves, she looks at her phone and sees the text message from Andre.

Two houses down.

She looks up from her phone and surveys the street. She sees headlights flash once as she steps away from the porch and into the moonlight. As she had originally intended, she presses on toward the police cruiser parked in front of her home instead of toward the flashing headlights.

When she reaches the car, she sees the peaceful image of a grown man, completely relaxed and vulnerable. She looks down at his lock to ensure that he has locked himself inside. When the poor guy comes to, he's gonna wake up in a panic, she thinks. She plans to be back by then to serve him coffee in the morning with a warm, reassuring smile and to remind him that his long work hours no doubt are to blame for his exhaustion.

She continues toward the flashing headlights and hears the doors to Andre's Dodge Challenger unlock. The car is black with darkly tinted windows and black rims to match. This car is made for their mission. Reaching for the door handle, she slides inside to see a smirking Andre.

"Damn, you look sexy in those pants," he smiles.

She can't help but blush at the dimple that appears on his right cheek.

"I'm not meant to be sexy. Did you bring the two dog bones like I asked you?"

"Yeah. They're in the backseat."

"OK, good. We are going to need them."

Sitting back in the plush leather passenger seat, she holds her phone and gloves in her lap and belts herself in.

"Pull out slowly, until we get to the end of the block. I will tell you where to go from there."

Andre shifts into drive and they begin rolling slowly down the street. Passing the police cruiser, Naomi looks in on the sleeping officer. See you in a few hours, Officer Carter, she thinks.

Parked one house down from the Greeley residence, Naomi and Andre sit in the car in silence. The tension in the air is almost stifling. She turns to look at Andre, who is staring straight ahead.

His head turns and he looks at her.

"Are you sure you want to do this?" he asks.

"Yes. This is the only chance I have to get the answers I need and the justice that my best friend in the whole world deserves." The determination in her voice rings loud.

Andre leans in and catches her lips in his.

Startled, she softens and gives in to the taste of his lips. Their kiss deepens, and Naomi feels Andre's hand on her thigh. She breaks their lips apart.

"Some other time, I am sure." She smiles and moves her body away from his, grabbing his hand and placing it back on his own lap.

Stretching her arms and sliding on her gloves, she speaks.

"Grab the bones from the back," she commands as she reaches for the door handle.

Andre slides on his own gloves, reaches in the back seat, and breaks open the fresh pack of extra-large dog bones.

Standing on the passenger side of the car, Naomi eyes the branch hanging in front of her, making sure it obscures the security camera's view of their car. Their arrival and departure have to be smooth, and their identities can't be compromised. She looks to her left and impatiently waits for Andre, who has yet to emerge from the vehicle. She briefly wonders how long it could possibly take to remove dog bones from a package.

They can't stand on the street for long. The neighbors here keep a close watch on each other's homes. Plus, some of them are just plain nosy. Just as her patience runs out, Andre rises from the car with a reluctant smile.

"Damn things are hard to unwrap. Had to take my knife to it; the plastic is so thick."

"Follow me," she says urgently, briefly annoyed that he didn't unwrap the dog bones ahead of time.

She turns away from the security camera that she knows is pointed in their direction and moves six bushes down, four bushes away from being in view of the next camera, and almost in view of the neighbor's window. She slides her body between the bushes and crouches down.

"Sebastian? Goldene?" she whispers for the dogs.

She can feel Andre's leg against the back of hers. They don't hear a sound.

"Goldene? Sebastian?" Her whisper is a little louder.

Andre adjusts his stance on the ground beneath their feet.

"Hand me a bone," Naomi says, reaching her hand up to take it from Andre. She holds the bone out in front of her through the fence.

"Sebastian! Here, Sebastian!" she beckons with increasing urgency.

Just then, the ground begins to move and a dog begins barking wildly. Cleary recognizing her scent, Sebastian, the chocolate Labrador, licks the end of the bone as his tail wags. Moments later, a beautiful golden retriever joins them.

"Hi there, Goldene," Naomi coos warmly, reaching her other hand up and accepting a second bone from Andre. Rather than lick the bone like her canine counterpart, Goldene sinks her teeth eagerly into the end of her bone and grunts.

Naomi smiles with relief and then stands. She moves to the right, three fence posts from where the two satisfied dogs are lying. With both hands, she pulls up forcefully on the metal post, wiggling it free from the top and bottom supports. Hiding the post within the bushes, she turns to face Andre.

"You ready?"

He nods his head in astonishment.

She turns sideways and lifts her leg through the opening that she created, and Andre quickly follows suit.

CHAPTER 15

They reach the side of the two-story, nine-bedroom, Colonial masterpiece. Even up close, the finishing touches are impeccable.

Naomi says a silent prayer that Michelle's emergency key is still hidden within the same secret "rock." She bends down to feel for the fake, plastic rock, which looks almost identical to all the others. As her hands search, she feels Andre hovering over her. He's trying to see what she's doing. After a few more moments, she gives up the search and stands.

"I can't find the spare key. We need to find another way into the house. Maybe Norman is careless enough to leave a window open or a door unlocked."

"Let's start with this one," Andre suggests, walking over to the window closest to him.

He pulls up on the window sash but there is no movement, not even a creak.

Naomi joins him as they move together toward the next window. This window is locked as well. They continue in silence around the house. When the last first-floor window is disappointingly locked, Naomi speaks.

"There's a keyless door on the side of the garage that leads into the house. I know that code like the back of my hand and can almost guarantee it has never been changed. Norman kicked me out of the house once, and I almost went to jail. So Michelle made sure I had a way in: either through the gate or the keyless entryway door so she could have company on the nights when her loneliness ate at her. We drank, we talked, and once she slept, I left the same way I came."

"Lead the way."

They walk around the back of the house and emerge alongside the three-car garage. Naomi approaches the side door and enters the access code, punching in numbers she will never forget: Michelle's birthdate. A green light appears. Bingo.

She opens the door into a nearly pitch-black garage. The only light to guide her is coming from the moonlight shining through six windows that line the top of the garage. Stepping inside, Naomi waits for her eyes to adjust to the darkness before walking toward the door that leads into the home.

Towering over her, Andre leans forward behind her, apparently trying to see why her steps stopped. She feels him behind her but still doesn't move; she's waiting for her eyes to adjust so she can scan the area. She takes a few cautious steps. Her eyes have adjusted slightly, and she scans the room as best she can.

The first thing that catches her eye is something leaning against the far end of the wall. The length and shape of the object tells Naomi it's a shovel. As she moves closer to it, so does Andre. No one speaks. They're standing in front of a medium-sized shovel. The bottom of it is caked with dried dirt. Hypnotized by the thought that this shovel could have been the tool that helped bury her best friend, Naomi reaches out her hand to grab it.

"Nooo!"

Naomi jumps at the alarm in Andre's voice. She turns on her heels, knocking into him, almost losing her balance as her eyes frantically search for an explanation for his outburst.

"Don't touch anything that could be evidence!"

Still in a state of bewilderment, she nods her head slowly, realizing that he is one hundred percent correct. Her eyes move from his panic-stricken face to the door that leads to the inside of the house. But a thought strikes her, and she turns back toward the shovel. Pulling her cellphone from her back left pocket, she takes a picture of the shovel.

When her eyes trail to the door so do Andre's, and he takes a step forward. They reach the door quickly, standing side by side. Naomi can feel Andre's eyes penetrating her in the darkness.

"You ready?"

Feeling his glare, she doesn't turn to look.

"Ready is an understatement." Her tone is heavy with fury.

Wearing her gloves, she grabs the door handle to go inside. The knob twists with ease and the door swings open to reveal a semi-dark kitchen, illuminated somewhat by the moonlight and glowing, LED readouts on the stove and microwave. When no alarm sounds, Naomi knew her instincts were right: Norman's sense of invincibility would make him careless.

Andre grabs her arm. "There's no turning back after this point."

Shaking her arm from his grip, she steps forward into a kitchen that is twice the size of hers, with an island as big as the eight-person dining room table in her own home. Naomi always loved this kitchen, even though the only reason it stays so immaculate is because no one ever cooks in it. It's still beautiful to look at and admire.

Not focused on whether Andre is behind her, Naomi moves through the kitchen, guided by the small patches of moonlight that escape through the trees outside the kitchen window. She presses toward a swinging door that leads to the next room. The door creaks lightly as it swings shut behind her. Before her is a medium-sized seating area with a wet bar in the corner.

Naomi looks around intently, hoping to find something besides the shovel to incriminate Norman. Walking through the room, allowing her eyes to slowly inventory every object, she spots two small, empty drinking glasses on the wet bar. As she walks toward the wet bar, she hears the swinging door creak. It's Andre.

"I went around the other side of the kitchen and walked through the foyer. There were some stairs leading upstairs and a living room full of antiques. Nothing out of the ordinary."

She doesn't turn to face him. Her eyes are still fixed on the two glasses. Fingerprints. Naomi turns to face Andre.

"We need something from the kitchen."

Surveying his body, she notices not just his muscular physique but also that he is still wearing his black leather gloves from the car. She steps toward him. When she gets close enough, her hand grazes his chest. Feeling the thump of his heart, she removes her hand.

"I want to take the glasses on the wet bar for fingerprints. I guarantee you they'll match the ones on that shovel in the garage. We need evidence."

Her body brushes past his, and they pause for a few seconds—long enough to feel an electric shock generated by the chemistry between them. Naomi takes in a breath as the connection breaks and she gets closer to the kitchen door. Still feeling the heat from Andre's body, she stands in the doorway for a moment to absorb it. Then she steps forward, navigating her way with the help of the moonlight.

"There has to be a plastic bag in here, something to put those glasses in. Or we can find tape— leave the glasses and just run with the prints."

She turns in Andre's direction, and he immediately rushes her, pushing her against the extended island. Taking her in close, his lips nibble on hers. A groan escapes from her lips as her mind scrambles to find focus. Their kiss deepens and their bodies press together just a little bit tighter.

Pulling off one glove against the resistance of her body, he slips one hand into her pants and breaks their kiss.

"You are so smart," he says, massaging her and looking for fire in her eyes.

Her breath catches in her throat, her head falls back, and her mind goes blank with pleasure. He stops suddenly, a smirk spreading across his face as she lifts her head back up. He takes a step back so that her feet can touch the floor.

"Start looking for plastic storage bags, a pantry, tape if possible. Anything that will help us get the evidence we need," she says with an exhale.

Andre puts his glove back on while Naomi checks the drawer closest to her. Silver. The next drawer contains knives and miscellaneous cooking utensils. As Naomi moves around the kitchen, she can hear the sounds of Andre opening and closing other drawers.

Naomi approaches what appears to be a pantry door or more cabinet space, but when she pulls the handle, the room fills with light from a concealed refrigerator. Closing the refrigerator door, Naomi turns to survey the room through moonlight. Her eyes land on Andre's image as he opens the last drawer.

"Well, I found Saran Wrap." He grabs the rectangular box with a gloved hand.

"That's perfect. Now if I could find the damn pantry. I'm sure there are bags there."

Andre walks toward her, on the same mission; his eyes survey the room.

"There."

He walks forward with Naomi only one step behind.

Only a few steps from where they once stood, next to a double-stacked oven, is what looks like two cabinets stacked on top of each other. Concealed in the corner is a rustic brown doorknob that only Andre could see from where he was standing. He reaches for the handle and reveals a pantry that is almost completely bare. On a shelf is a box of trash bags, some lidless pieces of Tupperware, what looks to be a bag of flour or sugar, and boxes of freezer and sandwich bags.

"Do you want a small or big bag? Looks like we have options," Andre says, opening the door wider. "Not even a damn box of crackers. I bet the refrigerator has a similar appearance."

The sound of keys turning in a lock catches their attention, as the noise echoes down the long, empty marble foyer leading from the front door. Grabbing Naomi's hand, Andre pulls her inside the pantry, placing his hand over her mouth, signaling for her to stay quiet. He removes his hand and closes the door quietly.

They hear stumbling, haphazard footsteps, as if someone is drunk and unsteady. Then they hear a giggle. Two distinct pairs of footsteps move through the foyer and into the kitchen. The light flicks on, and Naomi holds her breath and says a silent prayer. In her anxiety, her hand finds Andre's hand and she squeezes tightly. Their eyes connect, and Andre's speak to her in silence, reassuring her there's a way out of this. The tension in her shoulders eases briefly before more sounds of movement in the kitchen causes every muscle in her body to turn to wood.

They hear Norman's voice. He's rambling some gibberish they can't understand. Then they hear the now-familiar sound of the creaking swinging door, as a pair of high heels cross the room to the island.

"Awe, Norman, honey. Let me get you something. You are going to hate the hangover in the morning," a woman's voice says in what sounds like a thick French accent.

"There's a few glasses over there and some aspirin or some shit there." Norman's words are slurred but intelligible.

The heels clank in the direction of the sink.

"Oh no, wait. Maybe there is something in the pantry. That sorry excuse for a maid stashes pills in a gold container that she thinks I'm oblivious to."

The words are barely spoken when Naomi, trying to get up against the wall, stumbles and knocks one of the few items off the shelf. It falls with a clatter to the floor. Sheer panic courses through Naomi's veins.

The high heels clank toward the pantry door and it swings open, letting in light that reveals a black woman, about five-eight, wearing a black strapless bandage dress. One hand is on her hip, and her light brown eyes are brimming with fire at the clear intrusion.

Norman appears behind her only a few seconds later.

"Bitch." His one word comes out in a slur.

CHAPTER 16

Frozen in bewilderment and shock, no one moves. Naomi's eyes stare into Norman's with intense hatred. Her fear has been replaced with rage. Her eyes dart to the woman who opened the door, skimming her appearance with disgust. Then her eyes move back to Norman.

"What the fuck are you and your fucking lackey doing in my fucking house?" Norman's voice roars, his anger bringing about sudden sobriety.

Andre reaches behind his back for his 9 mm. Naomi catches a glimpse of the black gunmetal and her eyes widen in anguish; this is not part of their plan.

Norman and the woman, clearly aware of what Andre must be reaching for, take a step back.

"Now, wait a minute." There is clear panic in Norman's voice as it cracks.

The click of a bullet loading into the chamber is the only sound in the room.

The woman takes a few more steps back, her eyes wide with terror. Andre points the gun at her and without hesitation shoots the woman in the chest. The discharge of the weapon in the midst of total silence makes Naomi jump out of her skin. She stares in shock at the lifeless body on the floor. Her eyes move from the gun to Andre's face. His expression is maniacal.

Andre turns the gun away from where the woman once stood and takes a step forward toward Norman.

"Now, hold on," Norman's voice quivers.

Andre smiles menacingly as he takes another step to exit the pantry.

"I've been waiting a long time for this." He is speaking in a deep tone Naomi has never heard before. "Come on out of the pantry," he commands her.

But Naomi can't move. She can't think. She can't breathe. People aren't supposed to die tonight. She looks at Andre and then at Norman. Her eyes are wild with fear and her body is shaking.

"Come out of the pantry," Andre bellows.

Naomi takes a small step forward, unsure of whether or not her legs will support her body. Then she takes another until she is out of the pantry and standing beside Andre. Finding her voice, it comes out in a shriek of panic.

"What the fuck are you doing? What the fuck did you do?"

Norman stands still, seeming to hold his breath, as if the tiniest movement could cause the gun aimed at him to go off.

"Do you know how hard it was to get this man alone? And you played right into my hands, beautiful," he sneers.

Pointing the gun in Naomi's direction, he motions for her to join Norman by his side. She walks dumbfounded toward a man she thought she hated more than she could ever hate anybody, until now.

Their eyes meet as she joins Norman. She can see nothing in his eyes but fear.

"I will admit the sex was pretty amazing. Better than I imagined a thousand times before," Andre confides.

Andre steps forward and stands in front of Naomi, seductively tracing her lips with the barrel of the gun before moving it across her breasts and down her abdomen before removing it.

Her body is frozen; her mind is horrified by the sensation of the gun against her. Her children. Her precious children! She has to see them again. And James . . . I'll forgive him for everything if I just make it out of here alive, she promises herself.

Moving over to Norman, Andre's voice is filled with deep hatred and anger.

"And you, you fucking prick! I have wanted you dead ever since I started fucking your wife!"

A shriek escapes from the tightness of Naomi's throat.

"You fucking bastard!" she shouts at him, taking a step in Andre's direction.

"And what, my dear, do you think you are going to do about it?" he asks with a flash of intrigue in his eyes.

Locking eyes with hers, Andre swiftly lifts the gun and hits Norman over the head with one solid blow. Norman yells as he stumbles backward. He grabs the side of his face as a steady river of blood begins to flow from his head.

Naomi shrieks again, this time covering her mouth with her hands in horror.

"Don't worry, baby. She was nothing more than a pawn to me. You are the keeper of my heart and have been since the first time we went for drinks after work with Michelle and Amanda."

Naomi opens her mouth to speak, but no sound comes out. She's aware that her mouth is unbelievably dry. She looks down to her left at the dead woman as blood spreads across the white *terrazzo* floor. She raises her eyes to meet the crazed anger and intense passion in Andre's.

"I'm just doing what you wanted, baby. See, we got him," he says, aiming the gun at Norman. "Let me prove to you how much I love you by slaying your worst enemy. I told you I would do anything for you and I do mean anything. Don't you see I am your knight in shining armor?" His voice seems desperate for approval.

"Only the story didn't happen like you think it did," Andre continues. "You see, it was me who killed Michelle because she planned to tell you everything. All about how she was falling in love with me and leaving this asshole," he adds, shaking the gun in Norman's direction. "But I despised that slut. Yeah, she was falling for me, but she was also easy, and I wasn't the only man she would let seduce her after a little attention. My plan from the start was to find a way to make you mine. I only got with her to learn every possible detail I could about you. What you liked and what you didn't. When you were having a shitty day. Everything. I knew when it was a good time to flirt with you or cheer you up. And I loved that. Finding out about your cheating husband was a perfect opening for me. So when I tried to come clean about my feelings for you, Michelle said no. She said out of spite, she would tell you everything. I couldn't let what was developing between us go to shit so I had no choice but to take her out. I did it for *us*. And when she went missing, though it took you some time, I became your closest confidant and relished every moment of your neediness. But it's OK, baby, because all the evidence still points to this asshole. He'll get locked up and he'll never be free again."

"Wait a minute. I'm not going down for murder. I didn't love that bitch either but I didn't want her dead," Norman interrupts.

With another swift hit of the gun, Norman is on the floor.

"Oh yes you are, muthafucka! I'm going to make sure of it. There's only going to be one hero of this story and I guarantee it's going to be me!"

He looks from Norman to Naomi. Her eyes are huge.

"Oh yes, baby. Tonight, you lose your life as well, and I will emerge the only survivor to tell the story of my heroics. Of how I stopped a deadly fight after you called for me to rescue you from the grasp of your archenemy, and no longer will I stand in the shadows *waiting*.

"But, why?"

He grabs her by the hair, gripping her bun tightly and dragging her closer to him.

"Because you are never going to leave that asshole of a husband. He could fuck every bitch on the planet and you would still be by his side. Your loyalty is going to cost you your life because I can never have you. It was a mistake for me to ever think you would see me as the savior that I am."

He lets go of her and pushes her away. She trips over the dead woman and her foot slides through the blood, sending her to the floor. The blood is like oil on her hands and feet, and she struggles to regain her balance and stand. I'm not dying on this floor. Not tonight, she tells herself. Her first attempt

147

fails but she is finally able to right herself and stand. She sees Norman on the floor with blood covering his face, also trying to stand.

They are side by side again, but neither of them looks at the other. They are a ghoulish sight, Norman covered in his own blood and Naomi covered in the dead woman's.

"Let's take this party somewhere more comfortable, shall we?" Andre speaks, moving the gun from one to the other.

Norman takes the first step, followed by Naomi, then Andre with the gun pointed chest-high. They leave the kitchen and walk in complete silence into the small seating area with the wet bar.

Then Andre laughs.

"Anyone want a final drink before they take their last breath?"

"You don't have to do this. I will give you anything. I *can* give you anything," Norman's voice comes out weak but reassuring. "Name your price and I will make out the check right now."

"I want your fucking head on a plate!" Andre's voice is loud and crazed.

Naomi stands perfectly still, watching the interaction, trying to figure out how the fuck she is going to escape this. If she reaches for the mace clipped to her belt loop, Andre will surely shoot her.

Andre turns and looks at her and sees her eyes searching.

"Oh no, darling. There's no way out, except in a body bag, so you can stop those wheels from turning and have a seat. Maybe even a drink."

Her eyes land on his with defiance.

148

"I'm not sure why you think I'm just going to let you kill me. Norman is fucked up but you take the cake."

Andre approaches her so closely she can feel his breath on her face.

"Bitch, you haven't seen crazy yet," he whispers.

He pushes the gun into her stomach.

"I should fucking shoot you now and watch as all of your blood pours over the floor."

She hears the gun click. Naomi holds her breath and waits for the shot. She'll never see her babies again.

Norman moves, distracting Andre for a second. Andre pulls the gun from Naomi's gut and steps back.

"Where the fuck do you think you're going?"

Norman freezes, then says blandly, "To get that drink." Norman grabs a highball and a glass decanter containing brown liquid. He turns around. "Would anyone else like some brandy? It's from 1975, a pretty damn good quality. I only bring it out on special occasions, and since this is my last …" Norman trails off as he pours the brandy into the glass. "I might as well enjoy it."

With the gun still pointed in Norman's direction, Andre turns and looks back at Naomi.

"You might as well have that final drink, too."

Naomi forces herself to walk toward the wet bar. Norman steps to the side to give her some room and that's when Naomi sees it. Among the glasses and drink shakers is a small, shiny knife, probably for slicing limes.

In one swift motion, she slides the knife up her sleeve while grabbing a glass with the other hand. She holds the glass forward for Norman to fill. Norman tilts the decanter and fills Naomi's glass with brandy.

Naomi sips slowly, her head spinning. The brandy goes down hard, burning her throat until it hits the bottom of her stomach.

With his glass almost empty, Norman puts down his glass and the container of brandy and turns around to face his judgment.

Andre speaks, eager to stage the scene. "Sit over there in that chair."

Norman begins to move slowly in the direction of the chair.

With her glass still mostly full, Naomi sits it down.

Seeing that her hands are now free, Andre motions with the gun for her to come closer to him.

"Come here. You get to kill your greatest enemy. The man who hurt and abused your friend. Who lied time and time again, causing her so much heartache and pain."

Naomi approaches Andre without hesitation. She reaches up to grab the gun away from him, but he pulls his hand back.

"Do you think I'm stupid? I'll hold the gun, but I want you to pull the trigger."

Naomi steps in front of him then turns around slowly. He approaches her from behind and wraps his arms around her. His body presses into hers, and she can feel his hardness against her lower back. She shudders in disgust. Andre transitions the gun so that her hands grasp the butt and her finger is on the trigger, but Andre's hands are on top of hers.

"Now, pull the trigger."

Naomi's hands shake. Norman grips the arms of the chair, and stares at them with panic and fear in his eyes. Naomi examines him in this moment. She has wanted him dead or badly hurt for as long as she can remember, but right now he looks like a feeble, coward of a man. She almost feels sympathy for him. Then she thinks about the dead woman on the kitchen floor. She thinks about Michelle, and her anger rises.

"You're right. This asshole deserves to die. He may not have killed Michelle, but he caused her unending pain."

Her hands stop shaking momentarily, and she steadies the gun with Andre's help. Taking a deep breath, she loads the bullet into its chamber, and then she lets it go.

Before Norman can get out a scream, a gaping hole opens in his chest. The hit knocks him into the back of the chair. His mouth begins to move like he wants to talk but nothing comes out.

Releasing her hands from the gun, Naomi steps forward to watch his end. Norman stares at her while his mouth moves in silence. She watches as his lips stop moving and his stare turns cold, as life leaves his body.

"And now, it's your turn," Andre sneers.

Naomi turns toward the gun, now pointed at her. She walks up to her attacker slowly.

"Now, why would you want to kill me when I'm everything you want?" She places her hand on his chest. "There is nothing stopping us from being together. You have helped me in a way James never could. I'm all yours, and I'll never look back."

Andre laughs.

"You must think I'm some kind of fool. The only thing I have left for you is some dick."

Naomi drops to her knees and unzips his pants, pulling out his hard dick and looking it over. She has to buy herself some time.

"After this, the last thing on your mind will be to kill me."

He smirks.

She swallows him whole, never touching his manhood with her hands. The saliva builds up in her mouth, and her head moves effortlessly back and forth.

Andre exhales in pleasure.

She quickens her pace for a few moments then stops.

"Lie on your back. I want to ride you in your favorite way."

With the gun still in his hand, he watches her every move as he lies down on the floor. His dick is standing at attention as he reclines back.

Naomi takes off her black pants and straddles him. His manhood glides inside of her. They both exhale at the pleasure that consumes and connects them. Naomi moves up and down slowly at first. As she creates their rhythm, she watches Andre. He's still holding the gun. She begins to speed up, her breath getting caught in her thoughts as she fights back her own climax.

She hears the gun fall to the floor and Andre's hands swing around to reach her waist. He forces her body down harder against him, moaning in pure bliss. He sits up slightly to get a better grip. The new angle almost sends her over the top. She fights her orgasm with everything she has.

Naomi forces him back down and regains control of their rhythm. His eyes are completely closed now, and as she bounces, she can feel him nearing his own climax.

With Andre distracted, she has managed to work the tip of the knife to the edge of her sleeve. She rears upright, forcing his rock-hardness deeper inside her. She knows from experience he is teetering on the edge, and with one swift, powerful motion, she pulls the knife from her sleeve and pushes the blade into Andre's throat, slicing it open.

Blood pours onto the floor, and Andre's eyes are wide with shock. Naomi jumps up, kicks the gun across the floor, and watches as his hands reach in disbelief for his neck. She finds her pants not far behind her, and she reaches for them, watching Andre's last moments of life. Before she can get one leg into her yoga pants, Andre is dead.

Naomi pulls her pants up and, with an eerie calm, walks over to the bar and grabs her glass with bloody hands. She takes a huge gulp of the brandy and then sits the glass down. She turns back to face the scene before her, and tears begin to fall.

She pulls her cellphone from her pocket and dials 911.

"911. What's your emergency?"

EPILOGUE

The final smack of the judge's gavel signals that court is adjourned. Naomi, dressed in a simple navy blue pencil skirt suit, sits next to her lawyer. It's been six months since her ordeal, and despite passionate attempts by James to win back her trust and love, he failed.

The more he devoted his time and efforts to Naomi and the kids, the more his "side dishes" went out of their way to make their presences known. Late night text messages turned into phone calls in broad daylight, and on occasion, one of his lovers would have the audacity to show up in person. And Naomi often wondered if each mistress thought that she was his one and only. Did they all know about each other? Or did they each live in a fantasy world?

Not that Naomi didn't try. She and James tried hard at first. But as relieved as Naomi was to be alive, she couldn't bring herself to fully trust—or for that matter, respect—James again. Slowly, their fights dissolved into silence.

James moved into the basement guest room, and at that point, Naomi knew things were on the brink of failure.

When one of James' lovers ended up pregnant, it was the final push that Naomi needed to file the divorce papers without feeling an ounce of guilt. James was served at a Sheraton Hotel where he was staying during an away game. He sounded genuinely confused and distraught when he called after receiving the papers, and Naomi felt her heart threatening to break. But she had to move forward. Her children deserved better and so did she.

Now, sitting calmly with her lawyer, she watches as a few people sitting behind the wooden gate that divides the courtroom get up to leave. Across the aisle with his attorney sits James, looking both sad and angry.

Naomi pretends not to notice.

Her lawyer, Cynthia Coleman, smiles at their victory and rises.

"Well, I would say that was an excellent victory, being awarded ten million dollars, a beach home, two Range Rovers, your current home, plus daycare and other expenses for your kids . . . you didn't walk away with a bad deal."

"No, Cynthia. I didn't."

Exiting the courtroom, Naomi heads toward the door and the start of a new journey in foreign territory. She looks over her shoulder at the man she once loved—once gave her everything and all to.

He and his lawyer finally stand, and James turns around and notices her gaze. His face softens and there's a glimmer of sorrow, acceptance, and just a little bit of hope. He nods.

She nods back before exiting the courtroom. Once she reaches the glass exit doors of the courthouse, she emerges to a sunny winter day in Detroit. It feels like it's at least forty-five degrees, and the breeze is crisp and refreshing. A few puffy clouds dot the sky.

Naomi reaches the sidewalk and gazes upward.

A dove flies down from overhead and makes a few circles above her before flying away.

A sign from Michelle, Naomi thinks, letting her know that she is finally free and that it's OK for Naomi to rejoice in her own freedom, even though she has to experience the death of her marriage. She smiles as Michelle's smiling face passes through her memory, and she feels a small jolt in her heart.

The horrors of that fateful night at Michelle's house will be forever etched in Naomi's memory, but she knows she needs to let go of the past for the sake of her children and her own sanity. In the end, she came clean with the authorities and told them absolutely everything, from her personal quest to find her friend's killer to Andre's confession. Everything had gone horribly wrong that night, but Naomi managed to find the one thing she sought: justice.

She walks to the meter where her car is parked and sees she only has a few more minutes remaining. She presses the button on her key fob and gets inside, pausing for a moment to collect her thoughts.

When James and his lawyer walk by her car, she watches them from behind her tinted windows and ponders what might have been.

Putting her car in drive, Naomi sheds a tear for the past and looks now to a new beginning with a glimmer of hope in her eyes.

Tina Tennyson was born and raised in Detroit, Michigan. After high school, life took her to Dallas, Texas. In 2011, she obtained her bachelor's degree in early childhood education, and married her husband at the age of twenty-five. Her love for writing started young, and flourished over the years. It began with writing poetry, songs, and a few unpublished short stories. After working in customer service at Neiman Marcus for 6 years, Tina (also known as ShanTina) decided to take the first step to becoming an author at the age of thirty-one. This decision came after years of hesitation, but she finally took a step out on faith to make one of her biggest dreams come true. Her main goal as a writer is to make readers feel an emotional connection of empowerment. Her style of writing is captivating and will leave you wanting more. Prepare yourself to become completely submerged in the journey.

www.ingramcontent.com/pod-product-compliance
Lightning Source LLC
Chambersburg PA
CBHW070038260626
47159CB00005B/2071